Lost and Found

By
Dawn I Maith

Strategic Book Publishing and Rights Co.

Strategic Book Publishing and Rights Co.
12620 FM 1960, Suite A4-507
Houston TX 77065

www.sbpra.com

ISBN: 978-1-62516-867-2

Design: Dedicated Book Services, (www.netdbs.com)

For My Dad Gerry
18.7.32-10.8.11

Acknowledgements.

Special thanks to Ashley Paul Hairdressing, Gloucester for hosting my first book signing and for spreading the word.

Special thanks to Jan Dent who suggested I try writing in the first place.

Not forgetting my wonderful family and my friend Sally Robinson who proof read my work and, as ever, helped me when I needed it most.

1968

As the wet slithery body slipped from between her legs she sobbed with relief. She gazed through her legs, suspended in the stirrups, over her still swollen stomach, as she struggled to catch a glimpse of her baby.

"Let me see, oh please let me see," she pleaded. The mewling bundle was lifted away from her and wrapped in a blanket.

"You know that's not possible."

"Oh please, just one little look," her voice breaking with emotion.

The midwife placed a hand on her shoulder and smiled. "I'm sorry, love, but it's for the best. The new parents will be here to collect the baby soon. It's better for all of you if you don't have anything to do with it."

Lying back down, she let the tears come. As the medical staff delivered the afterbirth and stitched her episiotomy she stared at the ceiling silently listening to the baby's weight and measurements being recorded trying desperately to submit them to memory. The thought struck her that the small wound would be all that would remain of this day.

Eventually they took her legs down from the stirrups and brought her a cup of tea. With shaking hands she took the cup and sipped the sugary brew. The bundle had been taken from the room and all that was left was the blood-stained blanket lying on the hospital trolley.

"Nurse."

"Yes, are you alright?"

The student nurse stopped tidying the room and turned towards her.

"What was it?"

"You know I can't tell you that. I'm sorry."

"Please, just tell me was it a girl or a boy."

She shook her head as she turned away and continued with her task.

"Look, if I ask one question then you just nod or shake your head, then you won't have told me....Please."

She turned, uncertainty written across her face.

"Girl?"

With a quick glance towards the door she shook her head once and turned away again.

Letting her head fall back against the pillows she allowed herself a small smile.

"I knew it," she whispered. "A boy."

PART 1

CHAPTER 1

2011

She opened the front door and greeted him with a hug. "How are you sweetheart?"

"Hi, Franny, I'm ok thanks, knackered but getting there slowly. I never realized Mum had so much stuff, it's taking ages to sort it all out."

His Aunt smiled sympathetically as she took his arm and led him through to the kitchen. "I know, she never wanted to let anything go bless her. God I miss her."

"Mmm, I know how that feels."

Leaning against the worktop, she gazed out at the garden.

"Richard, there's something your mother asked me to give you after her death. A letter. She gave it to me years ago, when you were in your twenties and asked me to hold it for her."

"Oh...Ok. Sounds interesting."

"She gave strict instructions that I was to be present when you opened it."

"Blimey, that all sounds a bit mysterious."

"Why don't you go and make yourself comfortable in the conservatory and I'll bring the letter through and get you a drink."

Studying her face he frowned. "You mean a *drink* drink don't you?"

"Yes I do."

"Franny, why am I suddenly feeling a bit scared?"

Forcing a smile she gave him a reassuring pat on the arm, "oh for goodness sake, don't be scared. What could your mother tell you that would be in the least bit scary?"

"Nothing. I hope."

"Exactly. Go on; go through, I'll be there in a sec."

The letter was old and yellowed and the adhesive on the flap had started to give way. Turning it in his hands he saw his name written with a fountain pen in his mother's distinctive hand. He took a swig and slipped his finger under the flap.

* * *

My darling Richard,

Son, if you're reading this then I am no longer with you. I trust that aunty Franny is there. She will be a great support to you I'm sure.

Please know that your father and I loved you very much and rest assured that no child could have been more wanted or cherished. Unfortunately God saw fit to deny me the joy of pregnancy and as a result he sent us you instead. What I'm trying to tell you is that you were adopted.

The details of your birth as they appear on your birth certificate are correct, your birthday, age, place of birth, etc., but I am not your birth mother. We collected you from the hospital the day you were born; you were just a few hours old. We were told that your mother's name was Karen Barnes. She was only fifteen years old and alone. She wasn't able to hold or see you, and was told that I was the only mother you would ever know. I know we should have told you before but, every time we wanted to, I was just too frightened of losing you. I knew you'd want to find her and I couldn't bear the thought of you choosing her over me. I realized as the years went on that I was being stupid, but with every passing year it felt as if we'd left it too long. Eventually, we decided that this would be the best way forward. I admit it's the coward's way out, forgive me. We never meant to hurt you.

God bless you.

All my love

Mum xxxx

* * *

She studied his ashen face and shaking hands as he carefully, placed the letter on the side-table and downed his scotch in one.

After several minutes of staring at the floor he raised his eyes to meet hers. "Shit! You knew didn't you?"

"Yes."

"How long?"

"Since the day you were born."

"Fuck! Who else knew?"

"Both sets of grandparents. Aunty Lilly, Uncle Frank, Aunty Joan."

"Fuck!" He shook his head and stood up, frowning.

"It was always your parent's decision whether to tell you or not. It was none of our business, well, that is until now obviously. You were loved and wanted that was all that mattered."

"Adopted...Shit, I don't believe it....Adopted. But I looked so much like Dad."

His Aunt stood and placed her hands on his shoulders. "I know, that was the weird thing, no one would ever have guessed." He spun to face her.

"But why didn't they tell me, for fuck's sake? I had a right to know, this is my life. How could they have kept something like this from me for forty-three years?"

"To be honest I think most of us just forgot. You were such a happy family. After a number of years we never gave it another thought. It helped having you from birth though."

"My poor mother."

"I know, she was so desperate to have a baby bless her. When the chance came along to adopt she was overjoyed."

He raised his eyes to meet hers and for a moment she saw only cold bitterness.

"Not her, I mean my *mother,* for Christ's sake she was only fifteen. Fifteen Franny, how scared must she have been? My girls are older than that and I can't imagine them being able to cope all alone. Poor kid."

"That's very generous to think like that but try to remember she could have been an under-age prostitute or just an unlucky little slut. We don't know."

"How could you say that? Whatever she is, or was, she's still my mother. My birth mother. Mum was right. I will try to find her."

Easing him back into the armchair she placed herself opposite him on the sofa. "Richard please, give yourself some time to get over the shock. You need to gather your thoughts. It could take years to find her and even if you do she might not want to be found."

"That's fine. I'll understand. But I have to try," and all Franny saw in his eyes was determination.

*   *   *

Her phone chirped to signal a text. *Is it ok if I pop over?x* She smiled and instantly text back. *Fine let yourself in x.*

The shift had been hell and she was feeling exhausted, but the thought of seeing Richard perked her up. She quickly shed her uniform and jumped into the shower.

As she was wrapping the bath sheet around herself, she heard his key in the lock. "I'm in the bathroom, come up," she called.

"Ok, just gonna grab a drink."

She was just combing out her wet hair as he appeared in the bedroom doorway. His face was grey and drawn and he had what looked like a triple scotch in his hand.

"Hi."

"Hi."

"You ok? Has something happened?"

"You could say that."

Sitting on the bed she patted the space next to her. "Talk to me."

"I saw Franny today."

"How was she?"

"Ok."

"And?"

"She gave me this."

He handed her the letter. She took it and began to read as he knocked back half the scotch.

Eventually she looked up, her eyes wide and her mouth open.

"Fucking hell!"

"Pretty much sums it up."

"Shit, I don't know what to say. You must be totally stunned."

"Uh-huh."

She placed the letter back in the envelope and took his hand.

"Babe....I don't know what to say."

"That's ok. There's not much to say is there? Basically, my parents lied to me. My family lied to me. And everything I thought I knew about myself and my life was a pack of lies. No biggie eh?"

She heard his voice crack as the words caught. "Look at me." He raised his head and she leant over and kissed him softly.

"You're still you and your parents loved you. That counts for a lot."

"I know. I'm just hurt and confused. In shock I guess."

She giggled. "Maybe a little pissed too I'd say?" She teased. He smiled back.

"Maybe. Could do with a little distraction therapy."

"You sure you wouldn't rather talk? I don't mind."

"No, thanks. I need to escape for a bit and focus on something else. You, in fact."

Taking his face in her hands she kissed him again, her tongue touching his lips as he opened his mouth. As the kiss deepened they lay back on the bed and as his hand pushed the towel aside he reached for her breast. Her nipple hardened in his hand as he squeezed. Moving his mouth to her neck he nuzzled her and she moaned softly.

"Are you gonna lose the trullies, Murphy or what?" She whispered.

"Good idea. Why don't you take 'em off for me?"

He rolled onto his back and as she straddled him she began to undo his shirt buttons. His nipples were exposed and she softly licked and kissed each one. Running her finger down the line of soft hair running from his naval she unhooked each button of his jeans fly and undid them one by one. She could see his hard-on pushing against the fabric and as she released him he gasped.

His hands were gripping each breast as his thumbs flicked and teased each taut nipple. Sitting up he took one nipple in his mouth as her hands took his erection she slowly began to work the shaft with one hand as she caressed the head with the other. A glistening bead appeared and she wiped it with her finger and sensuously placed her finger in her mouth. At no time did they break eye-contact. For them it has always been this way, sensual, intense and very visual.

"Do it for me babe," he whispered. She smiled knowingly and reached into the drawer of the bedside table.

Lying back on the bed she switched on the vibrator and began to work it between her glistening folds until she touched her clit and shuddered. Her fingers found her opening. He watched her intently as he worked his cock. As she closed her eyes he knew she was close. His tongue found her clit and gave it the gentlest of sensual touches. Her hips jerked up from the bed to meet him. "Oh Jesus. I'm gonna come."

"Not until I say so," he teased.

He placed two fingers on the very edge of her soaking wet pussy and felt her shudder inside. Painfully slowly he slid them into her as she panted and writhed beneath him. She was so hot and wet and he wanted so much to get inside her but they both knew it was better to wait.

As he lapped at her glistening lips he rotated his fingers so his palm faced upwards and as he bent his fingers he hit her g-spot and her world exploded. She thrust her hips onto his hand as she grabbed at the sheet, clutching it in her fists. Her breath came in short pants and her breasts heaved. She rocked her hips and he struggled to stay with her. At one point his tongue lost contact and he realized that she was too far gone to feel anything except his fingers inside her. He watched her as she threw her head from side to side, her hair sticking to her forehead and thought how gorgeous she was. Eventually her climax slowed and she opened her eyes to see him looking at her and she grinned.

"That was incredible. Thank you."

"My pleasure. You wanna flip over?"

Wordlessly she rolled over and thrust her hips into the air. Taking his cock in his hand he knelt behind her and guided himself in. She was unbelievably wet and he struggled to keep his orgasm under control. He moved his knees to the outside of hers and squeezed her thighs tightly together. The sensation always drove them both mad. She was so tight and hot he felt himself gasp. As he slowly began to move inside her he felt her body respond and sensed her climax approaching. Increasing the speed he lost himself to the sensation and let his body take over as he pumped his way to oblivion.

At last they both collapsed, sweating and exhausted. "God I really needed that. Once I'd read the letter I just wanted to see you," he confided, his voice thick with emotion. She leant over and kissed him softly as he buried his face in her hair and let the tears come. Eventually he calmed. "I'm sorry. I just feel so lost. Like I've lost my past."

"Babe, I'm not surprised. What a shock. I wish I could help."

He smiled up at her as he ran his thumb over her bottom lip. "You just did. More than you know. I just needed to see you...To talk, to feel comforted...I don't know..." She placed a finger to his lips. "That's no problem hun, that really worked for me too. I was hoping you'd come over. Today was horrendous at work."

"I thought it might be, did they give us any more staff in the end?"

"No, just two trained and two HCA's for twenty-nine patients. It was awful. I'm knackered."

"Shit. I expect you are after that, are you early or late tomorrow?"

"You should know, you did the bloody off-duty numpty."

"Oy staff nurse, is that any way to speak to your manager?"

She laughed and slapped his bare bottom as she made her way to the bathroom.

"Bite me."

"Ok, if you insist," and he chased her into the bathroom.

CHAPTER 2

The two girls sat next to each other as the bus pulled away. "Did you get that bloke's number in the end, Luce?" Kelly asked nudging her elbow suggestively.

"Yeah, but I'm probably not gonna use it."

"Why the hell not? He's totally fit and he blatantly fancied you."

"Yeah right."

"He *so* did. Alright then why would he give you his number if he didn't fancy you?"

"He was wearing beer goggles. That's why."

"Why do you do that to yourself? Stop it will you. You're gorgeous and loadsa blokes fancy you but you never give 'em a chance."

"It's difficult that's all, after Tom. I just feel a bit wary."

"I understand I really do, but it's time to get back out there. Just text him, if he doesn't fancy you he won't text back. Simple."

"True."

"Go on then."

She stared at her mobile for several minutes and eventually, having typed her message she held the screen for her friend to see.

Hi its lucy from last nite jst wondered if u fancied a drink sumtime? tb.

"Perfect."

"You think?"

"For fuck's sake girl, just send it will you?"

* * *

The ward was bustling with nursing staff, doctors, physios, phlebotomists, occupational therapists, porters and domestic staff all struggling to complete a list of jobs impossible to achieve in the time allocated.

Richard led the staff out of handover and gave them their patient allocations. He discretely winked at Sally as she walked past. In the six months they'd been sleeping together they had always made sure their relationship never encroached on work. As the charge nurse and ward manager, Richard had always strived to keep his personal life private and it had taken him many months of deliberation before he'd finally asked Sally out. Fortunately, she was both sexy and discreet.

He picked up the phone and dialed the extension for the hospital social work team.

"Hi, it's Richard, charge nurse on ward seventeen. Is there any chance I can pop down after work today and have a quick chat with someone about a personal matter?"

He listened for a few moments. "No, it's not about a patient; it's off the record. Just a bit of advice actually."

Nodding he smiled. "That's great, cheers. I'll see you about two forty-five."

* * *

Josh's phone chirped and as he checked the screen he smiled. Composing his reply text he read it once then pressed send. *Hi Lucy gud to hear from u a drink wud b gr8 how about 2moz?*

His stomach fluttered with anticipation. Within a few minutes his phone chirped again. *2moros fine wen n where?*

I'l pik u up if u like 8ish? Again the answer came straight away.

Ok 6 Summerton rd Norden behind the bus station c u then.

He grinned and nodded approvingly to himself. He'd never believed she would get in touch. She'd seemed a bit distant somehow; wary and deeply suspicious when he'd asked if she would like his number and he'd practically had to beg to buy her a drink. "Good job I like a challenge," he muttered as he turned the corner and headed to work.

CHAPTER 3

1973

Jack took her hand and led her into the bedroom. They sat next to each other on the bed and she smiled sheepishly. They'd been going out for several months and so far had only kissed. A couple of times he'd slipped his hand under her top and caressed her breast and she'd felt his hard-on pressing against her when they'd danced. This moment had been inevitable, and she knew without a doubt that she had to let him screw her, whether she wanted him or not. She had to let him have his way or she'd lose him and any chance of a future. He cared about her and was kind and trustworthy. He had a job and a decent family.

"You sure?" He asked. She nodded without meeting his gaze.

"Yes, I'm sure, but first there's something I have to tell you."

He reached to push her hair away from her face and nodded encouragingly. "Ok. I have johnnys if that's what's worrying you."

She shook her head. "No, it's not that, but that's good. It's just that I'm not like other girls."

Grinning he took her hand. "I already know that you daft thing."

"No, Jack. I mean down there." She blushed and he looked away.

"Oh ok, erm, what do you mean? Is something wrong? Are you ok?"

"It's just that I fell when I was little and hurt my....Well, you know. I have a scar, everything still works and all that. It's just a little scar that's all. In case you wonder what it is."

He visibly relaxed. "I thought you were gonna tell me something awful then." They both laughed. "Shall we get undressed and get into bed properly?" He urged.

"Erm, ok if you like," she blushed again.

With their backs to each other they undressed and slid into bed on opposite sides. She felt his warm skin against hers and shivered with nerves. He leant up on his elbow until his face was over hers as he slid his hand between her thighs. As he reached her soft tuft she shivered again.

"It's ok. I won't hurt you I promise," he breathed in her ear as he kissed her neck. She desperately wanted to tell him her secret. To own-up but she knew he wouldn't want her if he knew. Jack was kind and loving and if she wanted a chance at a normal life then she had to keep the past where it belonged.

"Open your legs a bit for me darlin'," he urged and she obliged, just a little.

"That's it, don't be scared. Just a little more." He pushed her legs open with his knee and pushed a finger into her. She gasped in surprise.

"Sorry, sorry, did I hurt you?" His face was creased with concern and she was overwhelmed with guilt.

"Not at all, I'm just nervous that's all. I trust you, Jack."

"I'll go gently. Is this your first time?" She blushed and nodded.

Keeping his finger inside her he took a nipple in his mouth and suckled hungrily. Looking down at her he looked concerned. "Is that nice?"

"Mmm, lovely." She lied.

"Thought so," he nodded smiling.

"Jack, have you been with lots of other girls?"

"Not lots. Like I said, but a few."

"Ok. I just wondered."

"I've been with enough I guess." he wiggled his finger around inside her. "They all like that with the finger."

"Do they?"

"Don't you?" He snapped, his face full of concern.

"Oh yeah it's lovely," she muttered reassuringly, turning her head away to hide the tears that were forming.

"You sure?"

"Yes," she gulped, forcing a smile. "It feels...Good."

"Here, give us your hand." Her hand was ice cold as he placed it around his cock and guided it up and down the shaft. "That's it, nice and tight."

He lay back and closed his eyes. "Mmm, that's lovely," he groaned.

She suddenly felt the overwhelming urge to run from the room. From the house and from this silly, boastful boy.

As she continued to work his cock she felt him start to shudder. He took her wrist and moved her hand away. Her mind wandered back to when she lay with Sam. How she'd longed for him and how gentle he'd been. It seemed a world away from the misguided fumblings of this boy. Sam had kissed her, deeply and tenderly as he'd explored every inch of her body. Slowly undressing her.

Jack's voice shocked her out of her daydream. Her eyes flew open. He was grinning at her. "Oh hang on darlin', stop or else it'll be all over before we've even started."

"Sorry."

"Oh no, don't be sorry it was lovely. It's just I don't want to finish like that."

Moving down the bed he pulled the covers back and spread her thighs. "That's beautiful, really beautiful."

She blushed again as she tried to pull the sheets over herself. "Please don't look at me down there."

"Why not? It's lovely. You've got as lovely pussy, all pink and wet."

"Not really."

"Yes. Really." He tentatively and softly stroked the episiotomy scar. She cringed.

"I have something to confess," he whispered.

"Oh?" He took a deep breath and gazed into her eyes.

"Look, Ka, I haven't actually been with anyone else. Not the whole way, you know, having it off properly. Just a bit of fingering but that's it, sorry I lied. I just wanted you to think I was experienced. Most of this stuff I saw in me brother's wank mags."

She sighed with relief and burst out laughing. "Thank God for that. I'm so glad you told me, I was so scared you'd be disappointed with me. You having been with several other girls and this being my first time and all." He kissed her deeply and hungrily, his voice hoarse with lust. "Me, disappointed with you. Are you joking? You're gorgeous."

"Kiss me again," she breathed closing her eyes and drawing his lips to hers, "and we'll figure the rest out as we go huh?"

His face lit up. "Really?"

"Kiss me."

They kissed and as their hands began to explore each other bodies she felt her arousal awaken.

"Can I lick you down there?" He whispered in her ear and she silently nodded.

As his tongue found her she felt a whole new sensation wash over her. As his tongue slid into her she felt her hips push forward and with each subsequent thrust she felt her body tingle and pulse. Suddenly his finger found her little, swollen nub and she exploded instantly letting all thoughts of Sam wash away.

"Oh God....Oh my God," she panted. Her eyes traveled down her body to his as he peered from between her thighs. He was grinning. She laughed.

"That was incredible. It was amazing."

Moving up her body to cover her he nudged her still hypersensitive clit with his erection and she began to shudder again.

"Hang on. I need to get a johnny," he panted desperately struggling to reach his wallet on the bedside table.

She watched through hooded eyes as he carefully tore the packet and applied the sheath. He lifted his eyes to meet hers and grinned.

Gripping the sheets she threw her head back and moaned as he drove into her. His member pushing into her eased her to new heights, and as she thrust her hips to meet his, he sank further and further into her.

"Jesus, you're so hot and wet." He panted.

"Fuck me, Jack, just fuck me. Please. Hard." Her hands clutched his arse as he buried himself inside her until, eventually, they collapsed. Both completely exhausted. Lifting up on his elbow he looked at her intently.

"I love you," he whispered.

She started to cry as relief washed over her. She'd been with someone and it had been ok. He hadn't known that she'd had a baby, her secret was safe. He'd believed her. Looking into his face she knew she would do anything to make this relationship work.

"I love you too."

CHAPTER 4

2011

He pushed the double doors open and approached the department reception. The woman behind the counter looked up and smiled.

"Hi, I'm Richard from ward seventeen. I spoke to someone earlier and they said it would be ok to pop down for a bit of advice."

"Of course, Simon's expecting you. Second door on the left."

"Thanks."

The social worker looked up from behind a pile of paperwork, his face revealing both stress and fatigue. Instantly Rick felt a pang of guilt.

"Hi, Richard, come in, sit down. How can I help?"

Perching on the edge of the tatty plastic chair, he smiled sheepishly. "Hi, I'm really sorry to take up your time."

Simon waved his hand dismissively. "No worries. We have to look after our own don't we? What can I help you with?"

"Erm...Well...A friend of mine, well, a colleague actually, has just found out he's adopted. Apparently his birth mother was only fifteen when she had him. He had no idea and his adoptive mother left him a letter to be opened after her death."

"How long ago was this?"

Rick hesitated. "Er...This week."

"Jeez. So he's dealing with grief and then this bombshell. I take it you, oh sorry, I mean he, is back at work already?" Simon smiled.

Rick grinned back. "Yes I am. Came back today."

"Ok, well the first thing is that I feel you need some more time off. Losing your mother is bad enough but the shock of this adoption letter must have really knocked you for six."

Rick ran a hand over his face and nodded. "Just a bit, yeah."

"Tell me if I'm jumping the gun here, Richard, but I'm assuming you want some information about searching for your birth mother?"

"No, you're absolutely right. I want to find her and I don't know where to start."

"Ok, well, we usually advise people to access several websites. I have a list here."

He handed Rick a leaflet. "Some sites allow you to leave a message which she can pick up if she's looking for you, but others help you to track her down and make contact even if she isn't actively seeking you. You have to be prepared for the fact that she may no longer be alive or that she may not wish to be contacted. There's a good reason she had you adopted and if, as your mother believed, she was only fifteen then you may be the result of rape, abuse or incest. She may also have a husband or partner that knows nothing about you and she may want to keep it that way. Sorry."

"Shit."

"Exactly. The phrase 'can of worms' comes to mind."

Rick felt the tension in his neck crank up a notch or two and he rotated his shoulders in an effort to relieve it.

"Look, take the info, take some more time off and have a proper think about this. You probably won't change your mind but it will help prepare you for what's ahead."

"Yeah, you're right. Thanks."

They shook hands.

"Pop in anytime, seriously. I'm happy to help or listen. Whatever you need, and anything you say to me is in strictest confidence. Ok?"

"Thanks, I really appreciate that."

* * *

Lucy saw the car pull up and felt her heart pound. In an effort to slow her breathing she placed her hand on her chest and closed her eyes. Despite her best efforts, as the doorbell rang she jumped and felt herself blush.

"Hi," he grinned.

"Hi."

He paused and looked down at her intently before smiling. "You look lovely."

"Thanks," she mumbled.

He took her hand and led her to the car.

"Where would you like to go?"

"Erm...I don't mind."

"Ok then, anywhere you don't want to go?"

She laughed. "Don't think so."

"Ok then, fancy a stroll down by the river?"

"That sounds nice."

They made their way into the city and towards the embankment. Once parked he helped her from the car, and held her hand as they walked towards a riverside bar. "You seem a little nervous."

"Do I?"

"A tad, unless I'm reading this all wrong and it's just that you don't like me and don't want to be here. Then I'll take you home if you'd rather?"

She stopped and turned towards him.

"I'm so sorry; I'm being a bit of a prat. I do like you and I do wanna be here, it's just...I feel a bit vulnerable around guys. I had a really bad experience with someone a while back and it's left me a bit wary. It's not you, believe me. I wouldn't have text you if I hadn't wanted to see you."

He smiled and let out a sigh. "Thank fuck for that. I was beginning to think I'd forgotten to clean my teeth or hadn't put on deodorant. It was like the lynx effect in reverse."

Laughing she reached up to peck him on the cheek and he grinned appreciatively. "Let's get a drink," she suggested as she slipped her hand back into his.

* * *

Rick spread the leaflets out over the surface of his desk and sighed. His mind was spinning. He re-read his mother's letter and switched on his computer. As he started to flick through the various web-sites he realized he'd been given a huge head-start by having his mother's name and his place of birth. Absently he wondered how his mum had gotten that information. Heading for the government web-site he began to look for all Karen Barnes' born in 1953.

* * *

"You're a bloody nutter." She laughed as she placed her hand on his forearm. Josh grinned back at her. "You know, strangely, that's been said before."

"I'm not surprised. My face hurts from laughing."

"You're just easily pleased I reckon, or very polite. Fancy another drink?"

"Let me get 'em." She stood and reached for her bag.

"No, it's fine, I'll get 'em. You're my guest."

As he made his way to the bar she smiled again. He was so nice and incredibly funny. She didn't really believe all the stories he told about the escapades he'd gotten up to. The things he'd seen going on in the back of the limo he drove for a living, or the celebrities he'd encountered at various clubs. But even with a pinch of salt, she was really enjoying herself.

"There you go."

"Cheers. No wonder you're hyper the amount of coke you've drunk tonight."

"True, true. Can't afford to lose my license though so it's caffeine for me tonight instead of alcohol."

"Seems to be having the same effect on you."

"Me? I'm pretty hyper anyway to be honest with you."

"I like it."

She gazed into his beautiful brown eyes and without stopping to think, she placed a hand on his cheek and leant in to kiss him.

He felt himself getting hard as the kiss deepened and her tongue found his.

Pulling apart he grinned sheepishly as she blushed.

"What you blushing for girl? That was lovely. Pity we're sat in the middle of a pub though."

She smiled as he took her hand and brought it to his lips. "Won't be sat here all night," she whispered.

CHAPTER 5

"Hiya," he called out from the hall. He could hear the TV and smell the dinner cooking.

"Hi hun, good day?"

Jack and Karen met in the kitchen doorway and hugged. "Not bad, same shit different day I guess. Kettle on?"

"It will be."

She filled the kettle as he slumped down at the kitchen table. "Seen the twins today?" He enquired.

"Yep, Kirst' brought 'em round this morning for a couple of hours while she went to Morrisons. Easier that way."

"I'll bet. It's bad enough when it's two of us and two of them, can't imagine battling the checkout with one of us and two of them. They're lush but shit they're bloody lively." They laughed as they sipped their tea. "Is Lucy out tonight?"

"Yeah, she's met a new bloke."

Jack frowned. "How old?"

"Stop it, Jack. Let it go. She made a mistake so let her move on and leave it behind."

"Fair enough, I just worry that's all. She's our baby and she's been through the mill."

"I know, but I'm sure she'll be more careful this time."

"You reckon?"

"Yes I do." Raising his hands in submission he nodded and leant in to kiss her.

"How long's dinner?"

"About twenty minutes, but I could turn it down,"

"Go on then."

She rose and adjusted the rings and oven temperatures before taking his hand and leading him upstairs.

* * *

The night air was cold after the warmth of the bar. He pulled her body close to him as they walked slowly along the embankment. As they drifted into the shadows he led her over to the wall and kissed her deeply. She buried her fingertips in his short cropped hair and lost herself in the moment.

She felt a familiar tingle between her legs as her nipples hardened in response to his lips on hers. He rubbed his body against hers as she pushed her hips forward and started to grind against his hard-on.

He dropped his lips to her neck and nuzzled her as he slipped his hands inside her coat. His finger slid up under her skirt to her thong. "Oh babe, you are so sexy," he breathed. "I want to fuck you so much. Right here. Right now."

His fingers slipped past the thin fabric and as he eased between her lips he found her hot and soaking wet. Her breath was coming in pants now as he worked his fingers over her swollen clitoris.

"Oh my God," she whispered.

"It's ok hun, relax. No-one can see us."

As she shuddered he slipped his middle finger inside her. "Undo me," he breathed and as she lowered the zip his cock sprung free. She giggled as she took the shaft in her hand.

His deep growl rumbled through her as he leant into her neck. She worked him sensuously until he put his hand over hers to stop her. "Not in your hand, inside you. I wanna come inside you. Not all over you."

"What here?"

"Yeh."

He pulled a condom from his wallet and handed it to her. Carefully she rolled it over his throbbing shaft as he rubbed his fingers the length of her glistening wet opening. She shuddered and pushed against his hands as he worked her. Once the condom was in place he lifted her up and as she put her legs around his waist he slid himself inside her.

The shadows hid them and the area was quiet as he leant into the wall and eased her up and down his length. Struggling with the girth he felt her tense.

"Just relax," he whispered, and as he held her carefully and kissed her deeply he felt her relax as she enveloped him. He lifted her by the hips and eased her back down. Feeling her shudder and grip his cock with her wet pussy he pushed harder and faster. She came hard. Her head thrown back and her breath coming in gasps, and as he felt her pleasure, he let himself go.

* * *

She heard the shower go off and watched expectantly as her husband appeared in the bedroom doorway. He dropped the towel and proudly displayed his erect cock.

Karen smiled at him and lifted the quilt. "This is nice, the house to ourselves."

"Mmm," he mumbled, climbing in beside her and taking her nipple in his mouth.

He nudged her thighs open and his fingers found her. Without words she reached for the play gel and applied some to his fingers. As the cold hit her she gasped.

"Blimey, that's cold."

"Soon warm you up," he whispered.

He gently rubbed the lube over her lips and around her opening, making small circles with his fingers careful to avoid fingering her. She felt moist and velvety as the lube slid over her delicate folds. Breathing harder she took his cock in her hand and applied the gel to the throbbing head and shaft and caressed him lovingly with the silky lube. As he slipped his fingers into her he felt her bear down on him as her breathing changed. He saw the flush spread across her breasts as she closed her eyes and pushed against him. Using more gel she reached down to rub her clitoris as she came.

Easing his fingers out, careful not to stop her coming he quickly replaced them with his cock. Looking into each other's eyes, she worked her clitoris as he drove into her until they came together.

CHAPTER 6

He heard the front door. "Dad?"

"Hi, I'm in here." Quickly Rick switched off the computer and rubbed his face with both hands. His head was thumping and his eyes felt gritty and hot. His son entered the room and sat down on the sofa. Glancing at his watch he was shocked to see it was almost midnight.

"Good evening?"

"Actually, yes. Went out with a new girl tonight."

"What's she like?"

"She's nice. Sexy, fit."

Rick laughed and put his hands up, "oh mate, TMI, TMI. You might be talking about my future daughter-in-law there."

"Easy Dad. We only just met."

"But you did more than hold hands I gather?"

"Whoa, that's between me and my conscience. But let's just say, her body doesn't make promises she can't keep."

He looked at his son and smiled with pride. Josh, aged twenty-four, six feet four inches tall, heavily muscled, handsome. Good job, hard-working, never any trouble. He seemed to be the perfect blend of his mother's african-american heritage and his own caucasian looks. He thought how grateful he was to have him as a friend as well as a son. After the break-up Josh had decided to live with Rick whereas the girls had chosen to move in with their mother. The fifteen minute walk between his and his ex's house meant both parents saw all three kids regularly growing up but now the girls were twenty-two and nineteen he saw less of them than ever. He missed them. His thoughts turned to his parents and again he wondered how they could have lied to him every day of his life. The fear of being found out, the risk that some family member might let something slip must have caused unbelievable stress. Being a parent he knew he could never have lied to his children. The anger inside him flared again and he reached for a drink. He gestured to the bottle and when Josh nodded he poured two very generous measures and sat down opposite his son.

* * *

Lucy lay down on the bed and smiled to herself. She lifted her skirt and touched herself gingerly. She felt bruised and sore and as she explored herself she noticed spots of blood on her fingers. Grabbing the mirror she peered at herself. She had a small graze.

"Holy shit," she muttered incredulously.

The area was tender but not painful and although there was some blood it was not actively bleeding. She would survive. She lay back and smiled to herself as she remembered Josh's hands, mouth and pure brute strength as he had held her and entered her.

Her phone chirped. *How did it go?* It was from Kelly.

Gr8. He's gorgeous.

Kwl.

Her mobile beeped again.

Hi sexy, thanx 4 a gr8 time. Sleep well gorgeous. C u soon xx. She sat up and stared at the screen. It was Josh. Smiling she hugged the phone.

* * *

As he opened his eyes he became aware of her breathing. Flicking on the bedside lamp he saw Karen was grimacing and breathing heavily. "Are you ok love?"

She opened her eyes, smiled weakly and rubbed her stomach. "Yes I'm fine thanks. Just a spot of indigestion, that's all."

"You sure? Want some gaviscon?"

"That's not a bad idea. Go on then. It can't hurt."

Getting up from the bed he turned to her, "Is this the same pain you had last week when you said it was indigestion?"

"Oh, Jack, don't fuss please. I'm fine. It *is* indigestion."

"Ok, ok." He raised his hands in submission.

Making his way to the kitchen he couldn't help but give in to the concern he felt. She was blatantly playing this recurrent pain down and making light of it but her eyes told him that she was truly frightened.

As she swallowed the pink liquid, she took in his concerned expression. "Look, I'll make a doctor's appointment in the morning ok?"

"Want me to come with you?"

"No, I'll be fine. Promise."

He leant over and kissed her softly on the lips. "You better be."

He smiled as they cuddled down and turned off the light.

Once she heard his soft snore she rolled away from him and started to rub her stomach as the pain burned.

* * *

Elaine looked up from the pile of homework she was marking, to see her son coming through the dining-room door. "Hi Ma, alright?"

"Hi hun, yeah I'm fine. How's things? Dad tells me you've got a new girlfriend."

Josh smiled as he sat down at the table and began peering at the exercise books in front of his mother.

She nudged him to get his attention. "Well...What's she like?"

"Christ, you two are awful. I've only been out with her once."

"And?"

"She's nice. Lovely. Ok?"

"Are you gonna see her again then?"

"Maybe," he teased.

"Joshua...Behave." She playfully slapped him on the upper arm as she made her way to the kitchen.

He laughed. Although his parents were divorced they were like best friends especially where their kids were concerned. Generally speaking, you tell one something; you might as well have told them both.

"Yes, I'm gonna ask her out again. Yes, I really like her. Ok?"

Returning with two mugs of tea she sat down and took his hand. "I'm sorry, Josh, I don't mean to interfere. I'm just interested and want to be involved. I know you're a man but you're still my little boy really."

"Shit Ma, give me a break."

"Ok enough. You working tonight?"

"Yeh, pick up at nine. Going up west. Return at two. Doing some doorman shifts next couple of nights too."

"Oh, that's good."

"Yeah, good money too."

"Must make it difficult to see your girl."

"Ma, she's not *my* girl," he said smiling and shaking his head, "but yes it does. I can always take some nights off though, and we can go out to lunch so I reckon it'll be ok."

"I hope so. Working nights can kill a relationship."

"You don't have to remind me. I know why you two split."

His mother smiled ruefully. "It wasn't just his job, but you're right it didn't help."

His phone chirped and as he checked the screen he smiled. *Hi thanx 4 last nite n yr txt. Cn we meet up again soon? Xx.*

"Don't need to ask who that was. Look at that smile."

Without bothering to reply to his mother he instantly text back. *Luv 2 bt am working nxt few nites how about early evening 4 summat 2 eat or lunchtime? Xx.*

Evening better xx.

2 moro at 6.30? I'll pik u up?xx

Gr8.xx.

* * *

Mesmerized by the look on her son's face Elaine sat quietly, enjoying his expression as he smiled at his phone.

He felt himself getting hard thinking about Lucy's body; her pert nipples, her wet, tight, little pussy. Suddenly he became aware of his mother studying him. Hoping to get her to leave the room he looked towards the kitchen. "Er...Mum, any chance of a sandwich?"

"Yes, you know where everything is. Help yourself."

"Er...Ok. I need the loo first."

Standing and turning abruptly to hide the erection that strained against his flies he hurried from the room and up to the bathroom.

Leaning against the locked door he released his throbbing cock and took it in his palm. As he worked it he thought of Lucy and her beautiful little minge. In his mind he revisited each moist fold and as his climax approached he imagined sliding into her, inch, by tentative inch. He remembered the tension in her body as he entered her and the relief as she relaxed and took him in.

CHAPTER 7

Dear Mrs Millson,

I am trying to trace my birth mother who I believe to be called Karen Barnes. Born south London, 1953 and I understand this was your maiden name.

I was born in South London Hospital for Women, Clapham on March 19th 1968.

There are several women who fit the criteria and I am writing to all of you to with a view to finding my parents.

Please contact me at the above address if you have any information.

Thank you for your time

Regards

Richard Murphy.

* * *

The letters dropped onto the mat just as Jack arrived at the bottom of the stairs. Bending to pick up the envelopes he flicked through them grumbling. "Bill. Bill. Junk-mail. Shite."

Walking to the kitchen with the post in his hand he stopped and called over his shoulder. "Hang on, Ka, there's one for you here." She entered the kitchen looking tired and drawn.

"Probably junk. Open it up let's have a look."

He slipped his finger under the envelope flap and withdrew the letter. "It's shite, nothing to do with you. It's some bloke looking for a Karen Barnes who was born in south London in 1953. What a coincidence eh?"

Filling the teapot and sticking bread into the toaster she glanced over her shoulder at him curiously. "So why isn't it me?"

"Well, this Karen Barnes had a baby boy in 1968. This bloke's looking for his parents."

The smash of the teapot on the floor made them both jump as boiling hot tea spread across the floor. "Bloody hell girl, what are you doing?"

Her hands shook and her face was ashen. "Ka? Ka?... Karen, you ok?"

Unable to speak she sank to the chair as he mopped the floor and cleared up the broken china.

Eventually he sat down next to her and placed two mugs of tea on the table. Struggling to recover she smiled weakly. "Don't know what's the matter with me. Must be tired that's all." Placing a hand over his to reassure him she continued. "Sorry about that sweetheart. I'll get a new pot today."

"Sod the teapot; I'm more concerned about you. What just happened there?"

"I just lost my grip."

"Bull-shit."

"What do you mean?"

"That's bull."

"Are you calling me a liar, Jack?"

"You're hiding something, Karen, that's all I'm saying and I reckon it's to do with this bad belly that's been keeping you awake."

Relief washed over her. "That's it exactly, it's my stomach. I'm just worried it might be serious that's all. I'm just scared, sorry love."

"Just get to the doc's ok? It'll most likely be gallstones or something like that, whatever it is you can't go on worrying."

"Yes love, you're right. I'll ring at half eight for an appointment."

He kissed her on the forehead as he stood up to retrieve the toast from the toaster.

"I see a lot of women with gallstones at the hospital. Sorry, love but they're all about your age and build."

"I know."

"Just get to the surgery ok? I'll see you when I get in tonight but text me when you've seen the doc ok?"

"Ok love."

CHAPTER 8

1967

"Sam, I'm scared. My parents will kill me. They'll throw me out for sure."

"Then we'll live together as man and wife until we can get married."

"It's not that simple."

"Yes it is. I love you and you're having my baby. I can provide for us. Stop worrying."

"But I'm not sixteen till next year; they'll get the police onto you."

Taking her tear-stained face in his hands he kissed her deeply.

"In that case love we'll go away together and pretend we're already married and that you're older than you are."

"It's not that simple, Sam. What about my Mum and Dad?"

"Yes it is. I'll sort everything. I promise. You mean the world to me and we're gonna be a proper family. Your Mum and Dad will be fine once we're settled and the baby's here."

"I love you."

"I love you too."

* * *

2011

Sally yawned and opened her eyes. Rick was standing in the bedroom doorway holding the mail and frowning. "Not one fucking reply."

"Darlin' it's early days. Most people take years to find their birth parents."

"Yeah you're right. I'm just so fucking impatient."

"Tell me about it."

Throwing the envelopes over his shoulder he threw himself on top of her on the bed.

Laughing loudly he tickled her ferociously as she wriggled to escape.

"Stop…STOP!" She screamed.

"Cheeky mare, that'll teach you."

"Shush. We'll wake Josh if you're not careful."

"Hang on then."

He stood up and closed the door, proudly displaying his erection as it poked through the gap in his dressing gown. "OMFG is that for me?"

"Spread 'em, Goldie, I'm coming in."

Kicking the quilt off she spread her thighs as he shed the robe.

"I'm gonna fuck your brains out," he breathed into her neck as his hand slid down her stomach to the tuft of hair.

"Promises, promises," she giggled.

"Actually my dear, that's more of a threat."

"Bring it on…Come and have a go if you think you're hard enough."

"Ooh you cheeky minx. Is that a challenge?"

Before she could respond he had eased a finger inside her and slid down the bed so that he could gaze at her glistening folds.

"You are so wet. I love it."

"Mmm that's 'cause of you. You make me wet."

Leaning in he kissed the inside of each thigh, barely touching the skin. She shuddered and moaned.

Exploring her outer lips with his fingers and tongue he stroked and licked them from top to bottom before opening her with both hands to expose her engorged clit and soaking wet inner lips. Lapping at her from top to bottom she pushed her hips towards him. Careful to avoid her clit he slid his tongue inside her and reveled in the sumptuous heat and the velvety moistness of her depths.

Reaching into the drawer he brought out the dildo and used her juice from his hand to lubricate it. "Can I join in?" She panted.

"Be my guest."

Kneeling up she took the dildo and placed it on the mattress beneath her. As she used one hand to guide it in she used the other to spread herself, exposing her sensitive nub. Riding the dildo she rubbed her clit with her hand as he sat on the bed and watched. Rubbing his swollen cock and balls with his both hands they maintained eye contact.

"Bend over," he growled as he saw her nearing orgasm and placing his hands on her hips he slid into her and she gasped.

Slowly rocking together she let her hand slip down to her clit and as she circled the little nub he grabbed her breasts and pinched her nipples as they hardened.

Within seconds they had found their rhythm together and as he felt her pussy tightening on his shaft he let himself go.

* * *

As the front door closed behind Jack she flew to the bin and scrabbled for the letter. It was creased and stained with the spilt tea but she dried it with kitchen paper and spread it on the table. Her shaking hands traced each line and as the tears fell she knew without a shadow of doubt that she had to keep this secret from her family.

Sitting down with a blank sheet of paper in front of her she gathered her thoughts and began to write.

CHAPTER 9

As Lucy climbed into the car Josh reached over and drew her into a soft embrace. As they kissed and their tongues met, she felt a familiar moist tingle between her legs.

"Hi."

"Hi."

"You look gorgeous."

She beamed. "Thanks. Not looking too bad yourself."

"Why, thank you young lady. What would you like to eat?"

"Ooh, now there's a leading question."

Bursting out laughing he reached over to run his hand up her thigh. "Food first babe. I always work better on a full stomach."

As they pulled out into the traffic she felt a familiar thrill, the excitement of new attraction, but also the seeds of love taking root. Silently she chastised herself, determined that she wouldn't let her heart get broken again but fearing it may be too late.

* * *

"Ward seventeen, charge nurse speaking, how can I help?"

"Hi, Rick, it's Ali."

"Hi mate, what have you got for me?"

"Fifty-eight year old female, Karen Millson, collapsed at the post office this morning, query biliary colic. No past medical history, no allergies. Seen by the surgeons, she's got an IVI, NBM, awaiting MSU. Apyrexial, EWS 1 just because her pulse rate was up a bit but we think that was due to pain. All the usual bloods taken. The Reg will see her later. She's had IV paracetamol and five of morphine and she's comfortable now. ECG was done on admission to ED and was NAD. How soon can I tell them?"

"Er...Give us fifteen minutes to make up the bed ok?"

"Fine. Cheers, Rick."

Replacing the phone he stared at the note in his hand and frowned, remembering the name and date of birth. Eventually he turned to the nurse at the desk.

"Anton, you've got a lady coming into bed seven. She'll be up in fifteen minutes ok? I've written it all down for you."

The nurse took the patient details, perused them and nodded.

"Cheers."

* * *

Jack ran onto the ward breathless and flushed.

"Karen...Millson...Which...Bed...Please?"

Rick looked up from his computer screen and recognized the porter. "Jack, you ok mate?"

"Karen's my wife."

Standing he pointed to the board. "Bed seven mate, bay b. She's fine; say hello and pop back and one of us will let you know what's going on."

"Thanks mate."

Jack hurried to Karen's bed and collapsed into the chair. Taking her hand he started to cry.

CHAPTER 10

1967

She stood at the bus-stop and checked her watch again. The fog and damp had soaked through her thin coat and her hair was plastered to her forehead. He was now three hours late and it was pitch dark. Setting the suitcase down she realized she had to make a decision; to catch the next bus and leave, or return home to her parents and face the consequences. As a sob escaped her lips she turned and scanned the road for his familiar figure. At last she picked up the case and headed home.

* * *

Elaine's phone beeped. It was Rick. *Get the kettle on.* She smiled.

Twenty minutes later he strolled in through the back door and planted a kiss on her cheek. "Hi, how's things?" She asked as she filled the pot with boiling water.

He sat down heavily. "Mmm, well, have a read of this then ask me again."

As she read the letter he saw her face change. "Holy shit...Oh my God."

He laughed humorlessly. "Excellent use of vocabulary for an English teacher. I couldn't have put it better myself."

"Jesus, Rick, did Franny give you this? Did she know?" Elaine's eyes were wide with amazement.

"Yeah and apparently so did all the aunties, uncles, cousins etc. Fucking great eh?"

She placed her hand over his. "I'm so sorry. I can't imagine how you're feeling."

"I feel, numb, angry, betrayed, lost. I'm trying to find her you know."

"Really?"

"Of course," he replied, suddenly angry, "why wouldn't I?"

"Yeah, you're right absolutely. Sorry. How's the search going?"

"Well I've got the details of all the Karen Barnes born in 1953 and traced their marriage records. I've written to them, but no luck yet. She hasn't registered as looking for me on any of the specialist websites, which doesn't bode well. There's a possibility I may never hear from her if she chooses to ignore the letter."

"If. No. I mean when, you find her; I assume you'll want to see her."

"I think so. Well, at the moment I do but I guess it depends on her reaction."

"True. I can't believe it, everyone knew and not one person let it slip for forty-three years. That's some secret. And you look so like your Dad. That's weird."

"I know, might explain where Josh gets his height from though. I'm not short at five eleven but he towers over me."

"Could be, hadn't thought of that." She mused.

"I'll have to tell the kids at some point; although, I guess it will depend on whether she wants to see any of us. I'll tell her about them and take it from there I suppose. What do you think?"

"Have you thought this through, Rick, I mean really? Hang on before you have a rant and interrupt. Your parents loved you so much and it almost seems like you're trashing all that to catch up with a fifteen year old who just happened to be an incubator."

He stood up so quickly the chair toppled backwards. "Thanks very much."

She stood and placed her hands on his shoulders. "Listen, I care about you but it's my job to play devil's advocate sometimes. You have my support no matter what. Remember that."

"Franny doesn't want me to find her and neither do you. She's my mother."

His voice cracked and he slumped against her as the tears fell. "Oh hun, you just lost your Mum and now this. Sit down."

She led him back to his chair and rubbed his shoulders as he wept unashamedly.

* * *

The kiss was deep and lustful. Josh felt his cock straining to escape. His hand wandered to her thigh and she took it and moved it under the edge of her skirt up her leg. She wasn't wearing any underwear and he gasped as his hand met her soft moist flesh.

The meal had been lovely and although acutely aware of the time, he didn't want the night to ever end. Certainly, not this soon.

"Going commando, mmm I like your style. Good job you didn't tell me before we got to the restaurant. I would have been more interested in what was under the table than what was on it."

She grinned. "Thought it might be a nice surprise. Do you really have to work?"

He took her hand and took each finger one by one between his lips, his tongue caressing each tip. "Sorry babe, but I do."

"How much time have we got?"

"Not enough I'm afraid....Hang on I've got an idea."

Reaching for his mobile he began frantically texting.

After several minutes his phone chirped and a huge grin spread across his face. "Excellent...Right babe, my Dad's stopping at his girlfriend's tonight so how about you pack a bag. I give you my key and I meet you at mine when I finish?"

"Erm...Ok, sounds good."

They kissed deeply again and her hand brushed over his flies. He shuddered. "Oh fuck girl, I'm so close right now."

"In that case it would be really wrong to send you to work with such a dangerous distraction."

She smiled at him mischievously as she opened the zip and freed him. He threw his head back and closed his eyes, his breath already catching in his throat.

She took the tip between her lips as she worked the shaft with her hand. Reaching for his balls she rubbed them tenderly. Running her tongue around the throbbing head she sucked in rhythm with her hand and within seconds she tasted him as he shuddered and pumped into her mouth.

"Holy shit! That was fantastic." She smiled as she discretely wiped her mouth on a tissue. The taste of him lingered on her lips as he kissed her once more. Reaching into his pocket he gave her a £20 note. She frowned. Anger instantly rising inside her. "What's this for?"

He raised his hands. "Chill, it's cab fare. Listen, I'm gonna drop you at home. Pack a bag and get a cab. I'll text you the address and which bedroom is mine ok?"

"Thanks, but you don't have to."

"I know. I want to that's all."

The image of Tom pushing cab fare into her hand flashed into her mind and she felt the resentment bubbling inside. Holding out the money she looked into his eyes and took a deep breath.

"Look, please take this back. It's important. I know I'm being silly but I have a thing about it that's all."

Staring into her eyes he nodded once but didn't take the money. "Ok then, you get us a couple of bottles of good wine on me ok? It's Saturday tomorrow so we can have a decent drink and not worry."

She considered the suggestion and after several seconds she smiled. "Deal."

Her phone bleeped and as she checked the screen she frowned.

"Everything alright?"

"It's my Dad. He never texts......Oh shit. My Mum's in hospital, he says it's nothing serious, but I need to see her."

"Oh babe, I'll drop you. If you need to cancel tonight text me ok?"

He reached over and squeezed her hand.

CHAPTER 11

Jack sat at Karen's bedside and took her hand. He'd been with her on and off all day as his workload had allowed.

She looked slightly better, the tests had confirmed that she had gallstones and the plan was for pain control and surgery.

"Hello, love. How you feeling? The girls are on their way."

She smiled. "Oh, Jack, you shouldn't have worried them. I'm ok, just bloody hungry and the painkillers are making me drowsy."

"I know, but at least you'll get some sleep."

"Are you gonna cope alright without me for a few days?"

"Of course I am."

She leant over and kissed him softly on the lips. "I hate being stuck in here."

"I know."

She felt tears threaten and blinked to control them, noticing he struggled to change the subject.

"Eh, love did you happen to notice that the charge nurse on here has the same name as the bloke who wrote you that letter? The one about the Karen Barnes who had a baby. It was a local address too. I'll ask him next time I see him."

She sat up abruptly, her eyes wide, "Really? The same name, exactly the same name?"

"Well it was signed 'Richard Murphy' and that's his name, so it might be."

She stared into the middle distance, her face ashen. "You alright love? Do you need a nurse?" He started to stand but she placed a hand on his arm. "No. I'm fine, leave it, Jack. Really."

* * *

1967

She pulled her coat round her as she walked up the front path towards the front door.

Hesitating briefly she gritted her teeth and knocked.

The hall light came on and a man in his early thirties opened the door. He looked strained and his eyes were red as if from crying.

"Yes?"

"I want to see Sam Murphy."

The man gasped and frowned. "That's impossible I'm afraid. I'm his brother; may I ask what this is about?"

"I need to see him, where is he? It's important."

"I'm afraid my brother was killed last night. He was hit by a car in the fog."

Rose Barnes eyes widened in shock. "Killed?"

"Yes. We don't know where he was going but the police believe he was planning on leaving as he had a suitcase with him and all his money." Rose frowned as the pieces fitted together in her mind.

"I'm so sorry for your loss, may I come in? I think I know where your brother was going."

CHAPTER 12

2011

She opened the front door and reached for the light switch. The text had said it was just inside the door on the left and she found it easily. Putting her overnight bag down she walked tentatively down the hall. "Hello?"

Silence. She smiled with relief. She'd been imagining a change of plan where she'd open the door and his father, or even worse his father and his father's girlfriend were home.

The house was a typical Victorian semi, high ceilings, bay windows, original or at least a good reproduction fireplace. He'd anticipated that she'd feel uncomfortable so he'd text her with reassuring words and full instructions as to the layout and his bedroom, finishing with the words MAKE YOURSELF AT HOME!!

Pushing his bedroom door open she stopped and smiled, even without his directions she would have known it was his room. A waft of his Hugo Boss hit her as she entered and the weights on the floor in the corner were a dead give-away. She knew there wouldn't be any dirty underwear lying around. He didn't wear any, but there weren't any balled up socks either. Three walls were white with one wall papered in what appeared to be expensive black and silver wallpaper. Mounted centrally was a large plasma screen TV. His X-box and laptop sat nearby. Turning, she took in the major feature. The bed was huge, and surprisingly very neatly made.

"Mmm, not bad for a bloke," she mumbled to herself smiling. A small en-suite shower room led off and that too appeared to be clean and tidy.

Slipping off her shoes she went downstairs to the kitchen to put the white wine in the fridge and make herself a coffee.

Carrying her coffee back upstairs into the bedroom she laid out her short black satin nightie and robe, both more lace than fabric, and headed for the shower. He'd said he wouldn't be home until at least three am so she had plenty of time to exfoliate, shave, moisturize and generally titivate so that she would be ready and waiting in his bed. At the thought of this she walked over to the bed and flinging back the quilt she threw herself onto the bed and buried her face in one of the pillows, breathing in the smell of him, musky and sensual. Feeling the now all too familiar tingle between her legs as she grew moist she stood up, undressed and lay back down naked. Spread-eagled she let her hands find her nipples and a she pulled them, almost to the point of pain she felt her arousal blossoming. She bent her knees and let her hands slide down to her pussy. She was wet and swollen, her clit thrusting, desperate for his touch. As she ran the forefinger and middle finger the length of her lips she rubbed at her juicy opening with the fingers of the other hand. A moan escaped her as she came hard onto her hand. As the shuddering ceased and she removed her fingers she felt empty and dissatisfied. She wanted him, not this and as she headed for the shower she knew that she felt even hornier than she had before.

* * *

Franny opened the door and welcomed her guests with open arms. "Hello, hello, how are you both? Dinner won't be long."

"Thanks," they said together.

As they followed her into the kitchen she called over her shoulder, "Can you pour the wine, Richard, there's red and white. Who's driving?"

"Me," Sally replied, "I got the short straw."

Franny grinned at her, "Oh dear, make sure he remembers it's his turn next time."

"I will."

Richard returned from the conservatory with two glasses of wine and a tumbler of orange juice on a tray. "What's my turn next time?"

"To drive," Sally replied as she play-punched him on the arm, grinning.

"You could always stay over you know." Franny offered.

"That's a good idea. Maybe next time when one of us hasn't got an early the next day."

"Ok then, I'll remind you. Can you start taking some bits through for me? It's all ready."

They chatted throughout the meal until eventually Franny took his hand and looked him in the eye. "We've been skirting round this all night and I can't bear it any longer. Tell me. How's the search going?"

"Alas, nothing to report."

Her face dropped. "What? Nothing? Really?"

"Yes. I've traced and written to several Karen Barnes born in 1953 and nothing as yet. I'm hoping for a reply this week, even if it says 'piss off'."

All three laughed but as Franny and Sally's eyes met neither were fooled by his flippancy; they both saw the pain in his eyes...

"Please let me know as soon as you hear anything."

"I will, I promise."

"I assume you've told Elaine and the children?"

"Elaine knows but I'm not telling the kids until I hear something."

"Well, you'll have to tell them sometime surely?"

"Yes, but it's early days. I want to give her a chance, wherever she is, to come forward."

"I understand."

* * *

Sally pulled out into the intersection and switched on the CD player. Instantly he switched it off. "You ok?" She asked as she glanced at him, frowning.

"Not really. Do you think I should tell the kids?"

She sighed. "Is this because of what Franny said?"

"Mmm."

"Sweetheart, it's up to you. It's your decision."

"Yes but if I don't tell them aren't I being as bad as my parents?"

"Oh, Rick, hardly. Look, wait a few weeks and see what the post brings, then decide."

"Ok. I just hate secrets."

"I know."

* * *

Her phone chirped. *Am outside cn u let me in plz.*

Lucy had been dozing on his bed but as soon as she read his text all thought of sleep vanished. Jumping off the bed she ran downstairs and opened the door. The sight of her in black lace, warm and sleepy welcoming him home made the words catch in his throat as he took her in his arms and held her tight. "Mmm, I've been waiting for this all night."

She smiled as she placed her hands on his face and pulled his face down to hers. They kissed deeply and passionately. As they parted they pushed the door shut and he started to lead her towards the kitchen.

"How's your ma?"

"She's not too bad thanks. It's gallstones, painful but not life threatening. She's having an op tomorrow so I'll see her after. Dad will ring if there's a problem. Er, where are you going?"

"Gonna get a drink."

Pulling him back she smiled, "Upstairs already."

"Ooh, I love an organized woman."

As he followed her up the stairs he glimpsed her bare bottom as the little scrap of satin and lace moved just above him. "Stop."

"What's the matter?"

"I'm afraid I can't walk another step without doing this."

His hand slipped up the outside of her thigh and cupped her buttock. "Sit down."

"Let's go upstairs."

"Sit down. Here. Now. Please."

Silently she obeyed. He looked at her completely straight faced as she positioned herself facing him.

"Open your legs right up for me please." Without breaking eye contact she complied.

As her thighs parted his eyes fell and he moved down the stairs so that he was kneeling with his face level with her pussy.

A growl escaped his lips as he fell on her and traced the line of her lips with his tongue. She was soaking wet and hot. Easing a finger inside her he took her clit in his mouth and began to suck as he flicked her nub with his tongue.

Within seconds he felt her minge pulsing as her climax approached.

"Oooh sweet Jesus," she squealed as she threw her head back and thrust her hips against his face. She tasted so sweet he struggled to keep his own orgasm at bay.

He kept the pressure on until eventually she called his name. Lifting his head he looked at her. She was smiling. "That was my way of thanking you for earlier," he grinned.

"No thanks needed but that was awesome so I'm not complaining. Trouble is, I don't think I can walk, and I may have carpet burns on my arse."

He burst out laughing as he picked her up and carried her to the bedroom and sat on the bed with her on his lap.

"I have a secret to tell you," she whispered into his ear.

"Oh?"

"I masturbated in your bed earlier."

"Holy fuck! Let me think about that," he closed his eyes,"....Mmm....Oh yeah, that's nice...No. It's no good. I can't quite picture it, you'd better show me."

And as he sat on the bed and watched her, she spread her legs and took his pillow between her thighs as she fingered herself.

"You are so gorgeous, that's it baby; slide it in. That's it, nice and wet."

Within minutes she was working her clit on his pillow and as she came again he pulled the pillow away.

She opened her eyes and saw he was naked and very hard. "Fuck me," she panted.

"Already there babe," he growled as he covered her and nudged against her soaking wet folds. She gasped as he pushed against her.

"Tell you what, you go on top. Then I know I won't hurt you."

He rolled onto his back and she spread her thighs over his hips and carefully eased herself over his length.

She felt so tight and hot he clutched the sheet to stop himself from coming. As the seconds passed he felt her relax and as she slowly opened up to him he felt her take all of him inside her. Gradually she began to move more forcefully and as his thumb found her clit she threw her head back and thrust herself onto him in earnest. As he felt her judder he let go and drove into her.

CHAPTER 13

She had just finished tying the gown and struggling with the anti-thrombosis stockings when a male voice called out from behind the curtains. "Knock, knock. Hello, Karen, I'm Richard and I'm going to take you to theatre. How you getting on with that gown?" He called as he entered the bed space.

Unable to get her breath let alone answer she just stared, transfixed.

He was the image of his father.

"You ok there? You'll be perfectly fine, I promise."

She struggled to speak. "It's not the operation. I have something to tell you before I go."

Sensing her concern he beckoned her to sit on the bed as he sat on the chair next to her and took her hand. "Is there something bothering you? Do you want me to get Jack?"

"NO! God no."

He put a hand on her shoulder, alarmed at her response. His touch felt like an electric shock and she jumped. "Ok, love that's fine."

Slowly she raised her eyes to look at him. "It's you. I have something to tell *you.*"

"Ok."

"I think you wrote to me."

He smiled. "Did I? Then that must mean you were a Barnes before you became a Millson. I thought your name looked familiar. Sorry about that, I wrote to quite a few women."

She pulled away and stood up. Her hands were shaking and her voice cracked with emotion. "You don't understand. I wrote back."

He stared at her.

"I wrote back." She repeated. His eyes bore into her and he felt his heart pounding in his chest. He thought for one moment his mouth was too dry to speak and he was forced to clear his throat in an effort to respond.

"I heard. I need to know why you wrote back."

"WHY DO YOU THINK?" She snapped.

Tears began cascading down her face as she slumped to her knees. "It's me. I'm your mother."

Too stunned to even move Rick looked at the sobbing woman and the emotional reunion he'd envisaged disintegrated.

"You ok in there? Porter's here for you, Karen." It was Sally from outside the curtains.

"Can you come in here please?" He called softly as he stood up.

Sally's head appeared through the gap and as she took in his ashen face and Karen's sobbing she seemed almost unable to decide who to help first. Ever the professional, she went to Karen and helped the distraught woman onto the bed and by the time she had turned round Rick had gone.

"Tell him..." Karen gripped Sally's hands until her knuckles turned white.

"Calm down, sweetheart," she urged as she tried to release Karen's grip, "it's ok. Whatever's happened?"

"Tell him I'm sorry. Please. Just tell him."

"Who darling? Jack?"

"NO...Him, the nurse. Richard. Tell him I'm sorry."

"Ok I'll tell him. Are you sure you're happy to go to theatre like this?"

Karen's eyes were wide with panic. "I don't care what happens to me; just promise me you'll tell him."

* * *

Ignoring the amber light he shot through the intersection and accelerated. His hands felt slick on the steering wheel and he was sure he was going to vomit.

With shaking hands he fumbled with the key and pushed the front door open. Instantly, the door jerked as the chain pulled tight. "Fuck,....JOSH....OPEN THE DOOR."

"JOSH!" he yelled.

"Wake up," she whispered.

"What?... What's the matter?" He smiled as he took her in his arms and tried to kiss her.

"Josh there's someone trying to get in the front door."

He sat up just as his father's voice reached him. "Bollocks. It's Dad and the chain's on. HANG ON, DAD. Sorry babe, he's supposed to be at work. Wait here."

Running down the stairs hastily wrapping a robe around his naked body, he slid the chain back and Rick instantly pushed the door open and rushed inside.

"Dad, what's happened? Are you ok?"

"No I'm fucking not. I'm...I don't know what I am actually but I know I need a fucking drink."

Walking past his father to put the kettle on Josh heard the panic in his father's voice and saw the shaking hands and sweating face. Normally he would have casually reminded his Dad that it was only nine forty-five am and that coffee might be a better alternative but on this occasion he silently passed him a tumbler and the scotch.

* * *

"Karen....Karen, open your eyes for me. That's it, it's all over. You're in recovery now."

Slowly she opened her eyes and became aware of the oxygen mask on her face and the recovery nurse leaning over her.

As the mask was removed and a straw was placed between her lips she took a long drink of water.

"That's it," the nurse urged as she emptied the cup.

"Let's get you back to the ward. I'll ring the porter's lodge and let Jack know you're ok. He can meet you on the ward."

Staring up at the ceiling Karen's face held no expression. "Yes, that's fine."

"Are you in any pain?"

"No," she mumbled, still staring at the ceiling.

"Look at me, Karen," the nurse insisted.

Slowly Karen's eyes lowered and met the nurse's. They were misted with tears and such sadness. "Oh, love. What's wrong?"

Karen broke eye contact and shook her head.

* * *

Hearing the toilet flush both men looked up. "Shit, mate. I totally forgot you had a guest. I'm so sorry for barging in."

"Dad it's fine. Please, just tell me what's happened. Are you in some kind of trouble? Is it Sally? Just tell me," Josh pleaded.

"I can't, not yet. I'm sorry, Josh I just can't. I need some time to get my head around this. I'm not in trouble and no-one's ill or anything. Trust me."

Josh stood and put a hand on his father's shoulder. "Well I'm here if you need me ok?"

"Thanks."

Rick's mobile rang and having checked the screen he answered.

"Hi hun....No I'm not really....Sorry I left like that I just couldn't stay."

He mouthed 'Sally' to his son and Josh made his way up the stairs with two coffees.

* * *

She'd never known Rick to walk out of a shift, no matter what. His face had been grey and although he'd looked ill she knew whatever had happened wasn't physical. "Karen Millson gave me a message for you babe....Rick, did you hear me?"

"Yes," he replied softly.

"She said she was sorry. She made me promise to tell you."

"Is she back on the ward yet?"

"Yes. Clinically she's fine but she looks like shit and won't stop crying. We told Jack it's the anesthetic making her teary but he doesn't look convinced. What the fuck's going on between you two? What happened?"

For several seconds he didn't answer and when his reply came it was so quiet she missed it. "Sorry hun I didn't hear that."

"SHE'S MY FUCKING MOTHER! IT'S HER. SHE'S THE ONE," he screamed and hung up.

* * *

Josh pushed open the bedroom door and saw her face contorted with concern and embarrassment. She was dressed, and sitting on the edge of the bed. "I'm so sorry, I didn't want to intrude. Is your Dad ok?"

He shrugged. "I have no idea. He's freaked about something but he won't talk about it."

"Oh." She frowned.

"It's nothing to do with either of us or you being here though ok."

She nodded and allowed herself a small smile. "Thank God. I wanted to leave but I thought it'd be better to stay out of the way. My Mum's had her op this morning and I need to get to the hospital soon."

"Of course, I'll give you a lift. Thanks for keeping a low profile with Dad, you did the right thing. He'll calm down in a bit. He's talking to his girlfriend. She'll sort him out. He's chugging through the scotch right now so he'll either be chilled or pissed sometime soon."

She laughed and reached over to kiss him. "I didn't get a chance to say thanks for last night."

"You don't need to."

"No, but I want to."

He took her face in his hands and kissed her deeply and as she responded he felt himself harden.

He pushed her back on the bed and looked at her. "What?"

"It's not right you know."

"What? What's wrong?"

"Well for one thing you're dressed, and for another I'm not inside you."

His grin split his face and she reached up to kiss him again. "Better get this sorted then I reckon," she teased as her hands crept under his robe and grabbed his buttocks.

"Well, it's a tough job but if anyone can do it I can."

"I agree, Mr Murphy but I can't help but feel that after such a busy night you ought to have a rest and let me do the work. Wriggle up the bed and make yourself comfy."

He made his way up to the head of the bed and settled on the pillows, his hard-on making the toweling peak. She smiled at his erection as she slowly began to remove her clothes.

As each item fell to the floor his grin broadened and his cock broke free of the fabric. As she let her bra fall she took her breasts in her hands and played with her nipples as they hardened.

"JOSH!"

Her hands dropped and they both turned towards the door.

"JOSH!"

He hurried off the bed, stopping only to peck her on the lips and gesture to her that he'd only be five minutes. She sighed.

He poked his head over the banisters to see his father sitting halfway up the stairs. "What is it, Dad? I'm kinda busy here."

Rick looked at his son's face and took in the robe and the attempt to hide his groin and felt instantly guilty. He stood up and tried to climb the next couple of stairs. "Forget it mate, it's nothing. I'm fine."

"Dad you look pissed, hang on."

Josh headed towards his Dad just as Rick lost his balance and toppled backwards. A loud metallic clang reverberated through the house as Rick's head struck the radiator.

"Shit," he muttered as he lost consciousness.

Too stunned to move Josh stared at his father's body. "Dad...DAD!! LUCY! Quick, help me. Dad's fallen."

She threw the door open and saw Josh disappear down the stairs. Grabbing a sweater of Josh's and pulling it on as she ran, she followed him.

The man's face was white, his eyes were closed and blood was pooling under his head.

She stopped halfway down the stairs and felt the bile rise in her mouth.

Josh was knelt beside his father and was attempting to position the corner of his robe against the wound. She saw the panic in his eyes as he turned to look at her and knew she had to take charge.

She ran to the kitchen and grabbed the tea-towels from the radiator and knelt down bedside Josh and took his father's head in her hands and applied the padding to the laceration. She gasped, it was deep. He was breathing but he looked awful.

"Call an ambulance," she barked.

Josh patted the pockets of his robe and looked at her blankly. "My phone. Where's my phone?"

Nodding towards the land-line on the hall windowsill she instructed him. "Use the home phone, Josh. Hurry."

He stood up but wobbled as he made his way to the phone. It was only a matter of a few feet but she felt that it was taking ages for him to reach it.

As the seconds ticked by she heard him give all the right information but his father remained unresponsive and the bleeding continued.

Josh stayed on the line keeping the handset to his ear and stared silently at his father.

"Josh,… Josh, look at me."

His eyes moved slowly to hers. "Listen to me, he's gonna be ok. The ambulance will be here soon."

He nodded.

"Open the door hun."

He nodded again and opened the door just as the sound of sirens approached.

CHAPTER 14

As soon as Sally got the phone-call she ran from the ward and arrived in the emergency department breathless and anxious. Spotting Josh she grabbed him by the arms and peered into his pale, terrified face.

"Josh...JOSH!"

He focused.

"Oh, Sal, thank fuck you're here." He grabbed her and clung on.

"It's ok hun. How is he?"

"They haven't said."

Taking his hand she led him to the row of plastic seats lining the corridor and guided him down.

"Have you phoned your Mum or sisters yet?"

His head shot up. "Fuck. No. Bollocks."

"Listen, I'll go and find out how your Dad's doing and you go phone them. Don't tell 'em too much, I don't want them tearing through the streets like lunatics. Ok?"

As he stood a young girl approached. Her face was drawn and the oversized sweater was clearly blood-stained. She instantly took Josh in her arms as he slumped against her.

Sally tactfully waited until they separated. Catching Josh's eye she raised her eyebrows.

"Oh...Sorry. Sally this is Lucy, she helped me with Dad when I went to pieces. Luce, this is Dad's partner Sally. Lucy had to get a taxi while I went in the ambulance."

Sally smiled. "Why don't you take Lucy with you outside and make those calls. I'll see you back here in fifteen minutes ok?"

Taking Lucy's hand Josh nodded.

As she watched them exit the department she turned and headed through the doors marked 'staff only' and made her way to the nurse's station.

* * *

"Mum, hi. Please don't panic but I need you to come to the hospital. Dad's fallen down the stairs and cut his head open."

"WHAT?"

"I said.."

"I heard you son, it's ok, I'm on my way."

"Mum, please take it easy, it's not life and death he's just whacked his head so please drive carefully."

"Ok. Ring the girls for me and tell them I'll pick them up on my way through."

"Ok, see you in a bit."

Starting his second phone call he took a deep breath and tried to remove the alarm from his voice.

"Hi mate, Mum's on her way to pick you up. Dad's had a fall and cracked his head open."

He held the phone from his ear and grimaced as his sister's voice rang out. "Whoa girl, calm down will ya? He's ok, just knocked himself out."

She heard his sister's voice calming. "Ok, see you in a bit...No I'll ring her."

Hanging up he rolled his eyes and grinned at her.

"Shit, they bloody flap."

Redialing he repeated the information and the reassurances until, his youngest sister was calm enough for him to be able to hang up.

Turning to her he opened his arms as she walked into his embrace. Holding onto her for what seemed like an eternity he eventually let go and brought his face to hers.

"I don't know what I'd have done without you today. Thanks babe, I really mean that."

She smiled and reached up to kiss his cheek. "Oh hun, it's fine, I mean, it was nothing, I just did what anyone else would have done."

"I don't believe that."

"That's just 'cause you're easily pleased."

"Ooh, you cheeky mare."
They smiled and he leant in to kiss her deeply.

* * *

"Hi, Annie."
"Hiya, Sal."
"How's he doing?"
The sister looked down at the computer screen. "Well he's conscious, GCS fifteen, he's had an x-ray and some anti-bugs and they're sorting the wound. He'll be staying in but I reckon he's more embarrassed than hurt. Bless him."
They both smiled. "He's in cubicle four if you wanna go through."
"Thanks hun."
Sally hugged her colleague before heading towards the curtained treatment areas. She heard his complaints before she got close enough to open the curtain.
"... Absolutely not, I'm fine to go home. It's just a bump."
"I'm sorry, Rick, you're gonna have to self-discharge if you want to go home tonight."
"That's bollocks. Oh, Sally, hi love, tell him will you?" Bending down to kiss him she sighed with relief. "Jeez, Murphy you gave us a bloody shock."
She turned to the frustrated consultant who was endeavoring to glue Rick's head wound.
"Hi, Mack."
"Hi, Sally."
Taking Rick's hand she put her forefinger to his lips and leant down to stare into his eyes. "Now you listen to me. You're not going anywhere except the ward alright. Stop being such an awkward shit and use a tad of common sense for once will you?"
"Hear, hear," came the reply from the head of the trolley.
"Sal, that's ridiculous, I'm fine."
"I'm not arguing with you, Richard."
He sighed as the consultant winked at her over Rick's head. "Listen, I've got Josh outside and Elaine and the girls

are on their way so stop showing off and sort yourself out ok?"

"Ok," he conceded sheepishly.

* * *

Sally spotted Josh and Lucy and waved them through. "He's fine, whinging like mad 'cause he's gotta stay in tonight."

Josh smiled, visibly relieved. "Bloody typical. Thanks, Sal." He hugged her warmly. "No probs hun."

"Mum and the girls are on their way. I'll just text 'em that he's awake and moaning, they'll know there's not much wrong with him then."

Josh stepped away from the women and began texting.

"Sally?"

"Yeh."

"My Mum's in here at the moment. She's had her gallbladder out today so I'm gonna pop up to see her. Can you tell Josh where I am please?"

"Ok, no probs. What ward is your Mum on?"

"Seventeen."

"That's my ward. What's her name?"

"It's Karen Millson. My Dad Jack works here too. He's a porter."

Sally's face blanched. "Did you say Karen Millson is your Mum?" Lucy immediately picked up on the alarm in her voice. "Yes. Shit, she's ok isn't she? Have you heard something?" Lucy's face paled as she grabbed Sally's hands. Attempting a reassuring smile Sally responded. "No, no, she's fine, the op went well. Your Dad's with her at the moment."

"Oh thank God. I was planning to come and see her before all this happened."

Sally mind raced as she tried to make sense of the information. She felt her face redden and sweat break out on her forehead with embarrassment. Lucy frowned. "You ok? Has it all just caught up with you?" Sally raised her head and nodded.

"Mmm, yes I expect so."

She mumbled a goodbye to Lucy as she slumped into a plastic chair and started to think about Rick's son sleeping with his half-sister.

"Fucking hell," she murmured.

CHAPTER 15

By the time Rick was ready for transfer to the ward Elaine, Chloe and Amy had arrived and all three were fussing around him. Reveling in the attention he took their hands and kissed them.

Sally stood by the bed holding his hand and studying his face, desperate to tell him about Josh and Lucy.

"Blimey girls, if I'd known a little bump on the head would have gotten you fussing round me I'd have taken a tumble sooner."

"Oh Dad." The girls chorused as their mother pecked him on the cheek.

"Dear Lord, Rick, don't you see enough of this place already without spending your free time here?" Elaine teased.

"You'd think so wouldn't you?" He growled, "not my idea to stay overnight I assure you. I was hoping to have a chat with you tonight, about that person I was looking for."

Elaine frowned, "oh, *that* person...You have some news?"

"I have some really important news about *that* person to tell you too hun," Sally interjected, "but it'll have to wait I think. I'm gonna shoot off but I'll ring you as soon as visiting's over ok babe?" He studied her expression and the concern in her eyes. "Er ok, Sal, you alright?"

"Yes I'm fine just got something really important I need to tell you that's all."

"Do you need us to go, Sal?" Elaine offered, standing up.

"No, no, we'll talk later, honestly, you guys stay."

As she pulled the door closed she caught Rick's eye and in that second he saw panic and it made his blood run cold. He shook his head and turned his attention to his daughters. "Erm...What were we chatting about? You're supposed to remember, I'm the one with the head injury."

"You were on about a *certain person*. That sounds very mysterious. What are you two up to?" Chloe teased.

"It's nothing, Chlo, I promise, just someone your Mum and I used to know. Turns out she's a patient on this ward." Rick and Elaine's eyes locked as comprehension crossed her face. Raising her eyebrows she whispered, "*this* ward? *Your* ward?"

"Yes."

"Oh, ok, that explains what happened today. Shit, Rick, no wonder you...Well...No wonder you had a drink this morning."

He glanced at their daughters; they were both study-ing their parents in silence. Forcing a reassuring smile he reached for Elaine's hand and squeezed her fingers briefly. "Tell you what, I'll ring you later and we can talk ok?"

Elaine nodded, visibly shaken.

* * *

Karen was pale but looked comfortable. "Hello love."

"Hi Mum, how you feeling?"

She took in her daughter's bedraggled hair and the blood stains on the strange sweater.

"What the hell's been going on? Look at you."

"Oh my God, what a day. I've just come from the ac-cident unit. Josh's Dad fell down the stairs, well, not the whole flight just half but he sure cracked his head on the radiator. There was blood everywhere and he was out cold."

"Jesus," Jack muttered.

"I know, poor Josh. His Dad's ok though, just a nasty cut. Josh text me to say they'll be bringing him up to the ward in a bit. I heard the op went ok. How are you feeling? Really?" Her mother looked grey and tired and Lucy was sure she'd been crying.

"I told you. I'm fine," her mother replied with little convic-tion. Lucy and Jack's eyes met. "A bit tired I expect from the anesthetic?" Lucy suggested.

Instantly Karen's face contorted into a mask of rage. "I TOLD YOU I'M OK," she snapped.

Within seconds a head appeared round the curtain. "Everything ok? You need anything, Karen?" The nurse asked. Jack stood and raised his hands to placate the nurse as he ushered her out of the bed space.

"Jack? We have other patients who need a bit of peace and quiet, Karen will have to keep it down a bit or I'll have to ask to ask you and your daughter to leave. She's clearly upset about something and she needs to rest after surgery."

"Sorry, Bev, I'm really sorry about the noise. I don't know what's wrong with her. Do you think it's the anesthetic? She's really upset. Did the docs tell her something she's not telling me?"

"Not that I know of but if they had I wouldn't be able to tell you anyway, you know that."

"Yeah, sorry."

"Ring the bell if you need me but otherwise you might be better leaving her to sleep."

"Yeah, you're right. We'll say our goodbyes and come back later."

"Please."

Jack stood beside the bed and took Karen's hand. He met Lucy's eyes as she raised her eye-brows. Gesturing for Lucy to stand he said, "we're gonna pop off and get a cuppa whilst you have a sleep love. Ok?" His wife nodded once.

"Bye Mum."

"Bye love."

As they each kissed her she made no effort to respond other than to turn her cheek to allow them access.

* * *

"Mum, this is Lucy, Lucy this is my Mum; Elaine and my sisters; Chloe and Amy."

Still shaken, Lucy clung to Josh's arm as she greeted his family.

Elaine smiled warmly as she reached for Lucy and took her in a hug. "Oh child, you're shaking, are you ok?"

"Well, actually, my Mum's had an op today and I've just been to see her and well, she's not too good." Josh hugged her close to his body protectively.

"Oh you poor thing. What a day, you're having. Must be something in the water," she muttered meeting Rick's gaze.

She smiled weakly and shrugged. "I've had better."

Josh kissed her forehead as she offered her some reassurance. "That'll probably be the anesthetic right Dad? It does weird things to people sometimes."

His father hesitated. "Er...Yes, probably. Sorry to be so anti-social guys but I'm knackered. Could we call it a day?"

His visitors hastily got to their feet and said their goodbyes.

As soon as they'd left the ward he made his way shakily to Karen's bed.

* * *

Josh lay on the bed and took her naked body in his arms. "Oooh, you feel so good."

She smiled up at him. "Luce, seriously, you were amazing today, I don't know what I'd have done without you."

"Don't be daft, you'd have been fine."

He kissed her forehead. "No. You were there when I needed you." He kissed her eye-lids. "You were great, totally in charge and if it wasn't for you my Dad might have died." He kissed her lips. "I can't believe I'm saying this but I think I love you." He whispered into her hair.

She pulled away from him, her eyes wide. "What?"

Reaching for her he frowned. "I know it's very early for us but I do love you. You're gorgeous, funny, and sexy and I realized today how much I need and want you in my life. Sorry." He grinned sheepishly. "You're stuck with me."

Everything inside her head was screaming at her to back away, to slow things down, to give herself some time but her heart was running full pelt towards Josh and she knew which part of her she would listen to.

Shaking her head as she pushed herself against him she grinned. "Just for the record I need to tell you that I think we're both mad but...I'm afraid I think I love you too."

* * *

He stood at the entrance to the bay watching her face in profile as she stared motionless, at the ceiling.

Suddenly she turned and looked straight at him. He saw her gasp as she sat up.

Silently he approached the bed and drew the curtains. Turning to look at her he pulled up a visitors chair and sat down. Tears were cascading silently down her face as her hands gripped the sheet. "How are you feeling?"

"A little sore but ok thanks. What about you? What happened to your head?" She asked.

"Me?...I'm fine thanks, just a small cut." She nodded as he gestured towards the side of his head. "Only in overnight. Nothing to worry about." For a second she thought about Lucy's blood stained sweater and the story about Josh's Dad falling down the stairs. Shaking her head to clear her thoughts she instantly dismissed the story as mere coincidence.

They sat in silence for several long minutes until eventually he lifted his head, and looking into her eyes, he finally found the courage to talk.

"What happened, with you and my father? Who was he and why did you give me up?" She clutched a well-used tissue in her hand and dabbed ineffectually at her eyes, the tissue leaving white dust on her lashes. Silently he passed her the tissue box and she nodded her gratitude.

"His name was Sam and I loved him very much. We were due to run away together but..."

"But?" He breathed.

She smiled softly. "He never turned up, I always worried that he must have gotten cold feet or else his family found out and stopped him. I never saw him again. It broke my heart. I waited all day for him."

"That's awful. What a bastard."

"Oh no please don't think that. He was a lovely bloke, very kind. I have to believe something happened; he wouldn't have let me down otherwise. He was so handsome, you're very like him. It's uncanny." He blushed. "He worked in a bank and he'd gotten a transfer to another branch so we could start a new life."

"Maybe that was a lie too?"

She shook her head. "I saw the transfer letter; he'd gotten us a flat and everything. That's why it was so hard to accept."

"So why didn't you try and find him again?"

"Well, I went home to my parents and had to tell my Mum. She slapped me hard across the face, burst into tears and then hugged me. The following evening she went out and when she came back she told me that I would go to stay with my aunt and my Nan until you were born. Then I would leave you at the hospital and return home with my reputation intact. Either that or walk out the door and never come back. A simple choice that amounted to no choice at all."

"I still don't understand why you didn't try to find him, to get in touch. Couldn't you have traced him via the bank? You must have known where he lived."

She sighed. "My mother made it quite clear that I was never to see him again. It's that simple."

"But in subsequent years, you never even tried?"

"I met Jack and had a family. I was lucky to have been given a second chance."

"So Jack doesn't know?"

"Oh God no. No-one except my parents, my aunt and my Nan knew. It would kill Jack if he found out."

"But you're gonna tell him now?"

"What? Why?" Surprise in her voice, she frowned.

"I would have thought that was obvious." He reasoned.

She shook her head. "The letter I sent. You haven't read it yet have you?"

"It hasn't arrived yet."

She shook her head again and put her hand to her mouth. He noticed it was shaking. "It explains everything. My family must never know about you. Please understand. You must never contact me at home again, don't write, don't visit, don't call. You can use my mobile number if you need to contact me."

"*Need* to contact you? What about if I *want* to contact you?"

"Please try to understand..."

"UNDERSTAND?" He barked.

"I have a new life now, things are different. I am so pleased I met you but we're never gonna be one big happy family. It can't happen."

"That's it then?" He growled. She nodded once as fresh tears ran down her face.

"I'm really sorry," she mumbled.

Throwing the curtain aside he stormed from the bay leaving her sobbing.

Closing his side-room door he leant against it and as he slid down to sit on the floor he tried to calm his breathing.

"Fuck," he muttered.

His mobile rang. "Yes?"

"Rick, I have something to tell you."

"Sal, can't it wait till tomorrow. I just had a very *interesting* talk with my *mother* I feel like shit."

"Sweetheart you have a massive problem."

"Did you hear what I just said? I spoke with her."

"Yes I heard and what I have to tell you concerns her too."

"Ok." He signed resignedly, hanging his head in his hands, feeling his headache return with a vengeance. She took a deep breath, "God, I can't believe this is happening."

Recognizing the tone he sat forward. "Sally, you're worrying me. Spit it out."

She sighed and paused for several seconds. "Josh's girl-friend; Lucy."

"Yeah?"

"I think she's your half-sister."

"WHAT? Where you getting that from?"

"She told me she was gonna visit her Mum on our ward 'cause she'd had an op for gallstones. When I asked her Mum's name she told me it was Karen Millson and her Dad is the porter Jack. That means she's your half-sister and that makes her Josh's aunt."

"Fuck. Oh fuck. No way. That can't be right." His heart was pounding.

"Rick, it is. You have to tell Josh. You have to. They have to stop seeing each other."

* * *

Ending the call he pulled himself to his feet and staggered to the bed and sat down heavily. His head was thumping. The image of his son and his sister having sex flashed into his consciousness and as he felt the bile rise as he lunged for the toilet just in time.

Wiping the vomit from his mouth he looked at himself in the mirror. His face was ashen and sweaty.

He pressed the nurse call bell and began to open the plastic bag containing his blood-stained clothes.

By the time his colleague had arrived he was dressed. "Hi, Rick, you rang?"

"Paul, I'm outta here. Family emergency."

The staff nurse entered the room and closed the door behind him. "Er, I don't think so."

"Look I'm not arguing or pulling rank or being a twat I just have to go. I have to see my son. Now."

"Well you're gonna have to take your own discharge. I'll have to bleep the on-call and tell her."

"Fine, whatever you need to do."

"Are you sure this can't wait until the morning?"

"Sorry. No."

"Well at least let me do one more set of obs' on you."

"Ok. I can hang on for ten after that I'm going. Sorry to be a pain, Paul but I've got some serious stuff happening at home and I need to be there."

Raising his hand in submission the nurse smiled. "It's no problem to me mate I just need to make sure you're ok. Anything I can help with? Do you want me to ring Sal?"

"I just spoke with her thanks."

Fifteen minutes later he was in a taxi heading out of the hospital.

Chapter 17

"Dad? What are you doing out of hospital?"

Richard looked at the concern in his daughter's face and took her in his arms. "Sweetheart, I'm fine. The docs let me go."

"Really?"

"Yes. Stop worrying. Is Mum around?"

"Yes. She's in the kitchen."

He entered the kitchen to see Elaine nursing a coffee whilst gazing out of the window into the darkened garden. Hearing him enter she spun round, surprise etched across her face. Instantly she put the cup down and eased him into a chair. He looked pale and drawn. "Rick? What the hell? I thought you were supposed to be staying in overnight? Don't tell me you self-discharged? You could have phoned me to talk."

"'Laine I'm fine, my head's not the problem. I needed to speak to you face to face."

She closed the door and sat down next to him.

He shook his head and rubbed his face with both hands. "Shit, I don't know where to start." Pausing to take a deep breath he stared into space as he took her hand. "I found my mother."

"You said. She's a patient on your ward right? Who is she? Have you spoken to her?"

He turned to face her. "I've looked after her. That's why I walked off the ward. She told me who she was and I freaked."

"Oh my God, that's weird. What's she like?"

"Don't ask. She told me about what happened with my Dad and why I was adopted but that's not it really though. I was partially prepared for the rejection...Well I thought I was. Turns out it hurt more than I'd anticipated."

"Oh, Rick, hun, I'm so sorry," she stood and put her arms round him.

He started to shake his head. "Sweet Jesus it's worse than that. Believe me."

"Ok. So tell me."

He looked into her eyes and as he said the words he felt the tears fall from his eyes as he watched her face pale.

"Josh's girlfriend Lucy, the one we met tonight. She's my half-sister."

* * *

Josh kissed her hard as he ran his hand down her side, grazing her breast with his thumb. Lucy shivered. Sliding his palm over her hip he cupped her buttock and pulled her against him. His cock was already hard and hot and she gasped as he pushed it against her.

Feeling her nipples hardening against his chest he pushed his face into her neck and nuzzled her ear, his breath warm and moist.

Silently he pulled her on top of him until she was kneeling over his stomach. He sat up and took each nipple in his mouth in turn, nibbling and sucking until he saw her head fall back and her eyes close. Laying back he looked at her and smiled. His cock longed to push into her, to feel her hot, tight pussy swallow him. Inadvertently he shuddered and forced the image from his mind.

"Lift up."

Without a word she rose up on her knees and he slid down the bed until his face was below her. He could feel the heat from her and smell the musky sweetness of her as he looked at the glistening pink folds.

So very slowly he flicked his tongue along her soft inner lips. She responded with a satisfying moan and he smiled. "Mmm, we like that huh?"

She giggled. "S'ok I guess."

"Only ok? Well I'd better up my game then missy."

Reaching up he flicked her clit with his tongue as he slid a finger inside her. She moaned again. As he worked her clit with his tongue he turned his hand to find her g-spot. Easing a second finger into her he angled his hand and latched onto her clit, sucking the tiny nub. Instantly he felt her body respond as her pussy tightened around his fingers he felt her hips pushing against his face. Within seconds he felt her coming as he drove his fingers into her soaking wet fanny. She was on fire as she bucked and spasmed onto him, writhing and moaning.

"Oh, babe that was lush," she smiled down at him.

"You're lush."

"Stay there," she instructed as she turned herself around and laid down over him and took his cock in her mouth.

As her mouth met his erection his world exploded.

Grabbing her arse cheeks he thrust his face into her again and pushed his tongue up into her soaking wet opening. As his tongue entered her she pushed her hips against him as she slid her mouth down his cock taking as much as possible into her mouth. She gently caressed his balls as her tongue traced the head of his cock and sucked at him.

Feeling the heat and wet envelope his mouth and his cock Josh struggled to keep control. Within seconds he felt himself coming and as he felt her tight little minge grasping at him he let himself go, his climax slipping out of control as he pumped into her mouth.

* * *

"I thought we could send him to stay with your parents for a bit?" He suggested hopefully, the USA being his first thought and a good distance away. Elaine shook her head as she rose and began pacing. "That's ridiculous. He has work for one thing and he can't stay there forever whatever excuse we make up. And for another thing she'll still be here when he gets back. That's if he agrees to go at all that is."

"I know. You're right I just don't want to inflict this on him. He'll have to live with this mind fuck for the rest of his life."

"Poor boy. He's keen on her too."

"I know. And she's lovely."

She smiled at him and cupped his cheek, "it runs in the family."

A frown crossed his face. "Shit yeah, Christ, it didn't even register that I'd actually met my half-sister. She was there when I fell and at the hospital. Oh shit this is all happening too fucking fast."

"We have to tell them."

"No. My *mother* doesn't want her *family* to know about me. No way, no how."

"Then we have to tell Josh and get him to finish with her."

"Yes but then *our* family gets screwed over whilst hers remains untouched by this whole nightmare. Hardly fair."

"It's your call Rick. I'll support you no matter what you decide, you know that."

He smiled weakly. "Thanks."

"Drink?"

"Fuck yeah. Large one please. Should go down well with the pain-killers"

Having poured two large brandies she sat down opposite him again and waited. Staring out at the garden again he sighed.

"All this from one fucking letter. I wish I'd never read the sodding thing. What a mess. 'Lainey, I'm so confused. I wish Franny had burnt the damn thing."

"I know, but what about Josh and Lucy? They might have gone on to have kids and then what?"

"Well, we wouldn't have known any different and the kids would have been loved no matter what."

"Are you telling me you're gonna stick your head up your arse and forget all about it? What if they get engaged or married or want to live together. We'll have to meet her parents at some point and how long would it be before you and *mother of the year* freaked out and accidentally spilled the beans?"

"I know, I know," he whispered, "it's shite."

"We don't have a choice."

* * *

Josh heard the front door open and the voices of both his parents. He placed his finger over his lips to signal her to stay quiet as he left the kitchen and entered the lounge, pulling the door closed behind him.

Lucy sat at the kitchen table silently nursing a large glass of wine and a huge smile.

"Hi you two."

"Hi, Son."

"Blimey, both of you here at the same time. How come you're outta hospital Dad? You feeling ok?"

Calmly his father gestured towards the sofa. "I'm fine. Really. Josh sit down please we need to talk to you. It's important." Taking in their solemn faces he instantly sat down opposite his parents.

"Is everything ok? What's happened?"

Rick passed his son the yellowed envelope and sat silently as he watched his son's face.

Eventually Josh looked up, his eyes wide with shock. "Holy shit. Is this true?"

"Yes."

"Bloody hell, Dad, how are you feeling about that? You must be really shocked and upset. At least that explains the nine am drinking session and the drunken fall down the stairs. Dad I'm so sorry."

"Josh, there's something else, something that affects you. Directly. It's gonna be hard to tell you and hard to hear but we can't see any way out."

"You're scaring me. What the fuck? Just tell me will ya."

"I found my birth mother. Quite recently actually. She's a patient on my ward. I've looked after her. The day I came home was the day she told me who she was. She doesn't want her husband or family to know about me, which hurts, but it's not unexpected. The trouble is you already know her daughter. Lucy is my half-sister."

They all turned as they heard the wine glass smash.

* * *

Her hands were shaking as she fell to her knees. Struggling to comprehend she ran over the facts in her head as they cascaded over one another in quick succession. Her mother had a son. No-one knew. Josh's Dad was her half-brother. She'd been screwing her nephew. She was in love with her nephew.

As Josh rushed through the kitchen door he took in the broken glass and Lucy slumped against the units sobbing. She had cut her leg on the glass and was bleeding but seemed oblivious.

"You two. Out of the way." His mother barked.

Elaine took Lucy by the shoulders and helped her stand. "It's ok hun. Let's get you to the chair and sort out these cuts."

As Elaine tended to the wounds Lucy stared silently into space. The two men stumbled into the other room and Rick grabbed his son's arm. His face was scarlet with anger. "Why didn't you tell me she was here? You fucking twat!"

"I had no idea you were gonna tell me anything about her did I?" Josh retaliated.

Rick let Josh's arm fall as he sank into a chair. "Oh shit, poor girl. She obviously heard everything."

"I'm going in there."

"Josh, leave it." But Josh was already opening the kitchen door.

"NO!"

"JOSH!"

"Mum?" he whispered.

"She's not badly hurt; I don't think there's any glass in the wounds."

Walking over to the chair he hunkered down and took Lucy's chin in his hand.

"Babe?"

"Tell me it's not true. Please, Josh; just say it's not true. There's no way my Mum has a son. No way. We'd have known. It's just not possible. Just tell me it's not true. Please." She sobbed. He shook his head. "I can't," he whispered.

"No. I don't believe it. My Mum wouldn't lie like that." He ran a thumb over her bottom lip as the tears ran down her cheeks. "We're screwed baby girl. It's over for us."

"No, Josh, I love you, you love me. This can't be the end." She argued, pulling away from him suddenly angry.

Tears cascaded down both their faces as he took her face in his hands and forced her to meet his gaze. "We can't be together anymore. It's wrong."

"I don't care. We won't tell anyone. It's been a secret for such a long time, surely we can go back to the way things were. It's only us four that know and we won't tell."

"No, Luce, we can't. My Dad and your Mum know who they are to each other now and there's no way back. We can't be together and we can't have a family together and I know you want kids."

"I want you more." She whispered as she shook her head. "I want you more."

"Sweetheart, it's not gonna happen."

"Please?"

"Don't."

"Josh," she pleaded.

He stood and slammed his fist into the wall.

"FUCK!"

Taking his arm and wrapping his bleeding fist in a tea-towel his mother led him from the room.

Rick entered the room and sat down beside her. "I'm so sorry. I never meant to hurt you. I thought Josh was alone. He never said."

She met his eyes and noticed how similar they were to her own. She was still crying uncontrollably.

As if reading her thoughts he said, "we have the same eyes."

She attempted a smile as he continued. "I'm so pleased to meet you I'm just so sorry the way this has turned out for you and Josh. Believe me."

"I love him," she whispered.

"I know."

"There's no way we could...?"

"No."

"But..."

"Lucy, you're his aunt, by blood. It's illegal for a reason."

"I just want to be with him. Have you any idea what it took for me to allow myself to care again, to fall for someone else? You have no idea, no idea at all." She sobbed, her face in her hands. Passing her a tissue he tentatively placed a hand on her chin and lifted her face. "Lucy, I'm sorry to ask, it's the nurse in me I guess. Damage limitation and all that but...There's no way you could be pregnant?"

She sprung from her chair suddenly angry. "Pregnant? No I'm not pregnant, you're little scandal will stay under wraps."

Putting his hands up in submission he shook his head, "Hang on there, I wanted to be part of your family, it's your mother who has insisted that I stay away. Not me."

"Don't you mean *our* mother?" She replied caustically.

"This isn't my fault. I only found out I was adopted a few weeks ago...Fucking hell!"

Realization crossed her face and she sat down again. "I'm sorry. What a fucking mess. I just can't get my head around any of this...So what now?"

"Well, you go back to your life and I go back to mine and we never speak of this again."

"No. No way."

"Not my choice."

"You're my brother."

"And?"

"Don't we have the right to see each other?"

"Not according to *our* mother. No. Look I just found the letter she sent. She's made up her mind." He passed her the envelope he'd found on the hall table. "Anyway we can't have a relationship with things the way they are with you and Josh. It would be too painful for both of you. I want to be a part of your life but if your Mum won't see me how can it happen?" She read the letter and shook her head silently.

"Oh fucking hell. I'm so confused. What do I do? I can't un-hear this, I can't un-know this. How can I face Mum? What do I say?" She buried her face in her hands. He felt his heart breaking. Taking a deep breath he took her hands from her face and began wiping her tears.

"No-one can make that decision for you. I suggest you talk to her. Alone."

"Will I see you again?"

"I honestly don't know."

They stood and embraced awkwardly.

"Tell Josh..."

He placed a finger on her lips before she could finish. "Shush, don't, please. I have to live with the knowledge that I broke my son's heart tonight. Anything I say to him will only make things worse."

She nodded.

* * *

Elaine tried to control her son's anger but he was out the front door before she could reason with him. Hearing his car speed off she picked up her phone and began to ring her daughters.

CHAPTER 18

Mimi's mobile chirped, *where r u?* The text read.

At home u ok?

No need yr company. Professional visit

Ok.

C u in 10.

Running up the stairs she quickly changed into her working clothes and slipped a black satin robe over the top. She applied more lip gloss and more perfume before fluffing her hair.

Within minutes she heard the doorbell.

"Hi hun."

Without answering Josh grabbed her and kissed her hard. "Upstairs," he growled as he took her hand and led the way. She noticed the grazed knuckles and the blood-stained tea-towel as he dropped it on the floor.

Understanding the fury on his face and the urgency in his kiss she followed silently knowing that he would speak as, and when, he felt like it.

As they entered the bedroom he pushed her onto the bed and fell on top of her pawing at her bra to expose her breast. Taking the nipple he bit her hard and she yelped but did not resist.

"Take it off," he ordered.

As she unclipped the bra and her breasts were exposed he grabbed one hard whilst pulling at the other nipple with his teeth.

Lying on the bed with her arms pinned above her head she looked up at him as he reached between her legs, pulled her thong from her and forced her legs wide open.

He was mindless and totally focused.

With no hint of the gentleness he felt for Lucy, he thrust hard into Mimi making her squirm and gasp.

Well known for her taste in rough sex she felt herself becoming more and more aroused as he nibbled her already bruised nipples and thrust into her already stretched pussy. She knew better than to ask him to ease up. He was way past that point. As he forced further into her he felt her body yielding slowly but was in no mood to wait. She was hot and tight and wet as he forced his cock into her, and as he buried his face in her neck he wanted more than anything to hurt someone, anyone. He pumped hard and fast until he felt oblivion overtake him.

As he collapsed onto her he felt her put her arms around him.

"Get off me!" He snarled.

"Josh, what's wrong? I thought we were friends. Talk to me."

"You're a fucking whore, not my friend. What? You want paying now?"

"You bastard."

Realization struck him and as he looked into her eyes he knew he had overstepped the mark.

"Shit, Mimi, I'm so sorry, I'm such a prick. Do me a favor will you? Hit me."

"What?"

"Just hit me. Hard."

"Ok."

Her fist struck his face and he tasted blood in his mouth.

"Again." She punched him a second time.

"Again."

As the blows cascaded onto his face and the blood flowed from his mouth and nose he let the tears fall.

* * *

Lucy watched her father pull off the drive as he left to collect her Mum from the hospital.

She'd been awake all night crying with disappointment and anger.

Her mobile bleeped. A text from Josh. Her heart leapt. It was blank. She understood immediately, he was thinking about her but had no words to say what he was feeling. She felt the same and sent him a blank text back.

* * *

Karen was strangely silent throughout the drive home and despite his best efforts Jack was unable to illicit anything other than the occasional monosyllabic response.

As they entered the house he led her to the sofa and urged her to sit. As he brought the footstool and the remote he chattered away inanely as she gazed out of the window.

"You look shattered love. I'll put the kettle on and we'll have a cuppa."

She nodded mutely.

As Lucy saw the car pull up and heard the front door close she slowly made her way downstairs.

Entering the lounge she closed the door behind her and turned the key.

Karen's head spun round and as she met her daughter's gaze she blanched. Lucy looked furious, hurt, confused. Something was terribly wrong. As she desperately tried to second guess the cause Lucy sat down, took a deep breath and began to talk.

"I know about Richard, Mum. I know everything."

Karen's heart jumped and she felt herself blush as sweat broke out on her forehead and upper lip. "Richard who? What are you talking about?"

"STOP. IT!"

"Stop what, Lucy? You'll have to explain yourself."

"Oh, ok, we're gonna play that game are we? Well FYI, it won't work anymore, forty-three years is long enough, time to 'fess up and face the music *mother.*"

"Lucy I..."

"Your son, Richard, the one you had and gave up for adoption. I know him. My brother."

"Lucy listen..." She pleaded weakly.

"Oh no, *mother* you haven't heard the best bit yet. He has a son, a son called Josh. A twenty-four year old son called Josh. My Josh." Karen's eyes widened as realization hit her.

"Oh no, please no."

"Oh yes. I have been fucking my nephew, your grand-son."

Karen struggled to get to her feet but as she tried to stand her legs gave way and she collapsed sobbing.

"KAREN! KAREN!" The door handle rattled, "have you locked the door? What's going on?"

Both women turned in response to Jack's voice.

Leaning down to peer into her mother's eyes, her tone low and menacing, Lucy delivered the final blow.

"You have forty-eight hours to tell Dad or I will."

"No, Lucy it'll kill him. Please..."

"Deal with it...COMING DAD."

Casually unlocking the door Lucy threw her arms round her father and hugged him tightly.

"Eh eh, what's all this in aid of? Why did you lock this door? What are you up to?" He took in the thinly masked anger on his daughter's face as his wife struggled to get to her feet, clearly shaken.

"I'm fine, Jack. Honestly, no problem."

"So why was the door locked?"

"Oh, Dad," Lucy teased from the hall as she headed back upstairs, "we can't exactly discuss your birthday surprise with you about to walk in at any moment."

Jack sat beside his wife and held her tenderly.

"You'd tell me wouldn't you? If the doctors had told you anything bad. Please tell me what's wrong darlin'? You can tell me anything you know that."

She squeezed his hand as she nodded, knowing this was to prove a lie.

CHAPTER 19

1967

"You'd better come in." Standing aside the man looked unsure but let her in anyway.

She followed him down the hall to the kitchen where a woman stood at the stove stirring a saucepan. As she looked round Rose saw that her eyes were also blood-shot and teary.

"Mrs Murphy, I'm so sorry to intrude at this time but I think I know where your brother-in-law was going last night."

Placing a hand on his wife's shoulder the man nodded. "Put the kettle on love."

Once they were sat at the table Rose began.

"Last night my daughter came home with a suitcase. She'd been out all evening. She had been crying. It turns out she was due to meet a Sam Murphy and they were going to run away together."

The woman's hand flew to her mouth as her husband grabbed her shoulder. Rose continued. "She gave me this address for him and also told me she's in the family way, five months gone by all accounts."

The man frowned. "No, Sam would never get a girl into trouble, never, he wasn't like that..."

"And neither is my Karen, but there you are, it's happened. As far as she's concerned he let her down. She's all alone with this baby and no-one to take responsibility."

"Well what do you expect me to do about it? Sam didn't leave anything he was only nineteen."

"Yes well, my Karen's only fifteen."

"Oh dear God," the woman whispered.

The man stood up angrily and placing both hands on the table he leant down over Rose. "I don't know what your game is but you'll get nothing from us. You'd better leave."

The woman looked pleadingly at her husband as she placed a placating hand on his arm. "Please, Frank, just give her a minute."

He paused, then sat down. "Alright, one more minute."

The woman turned to Rose. "My name is Eileen and this is Frank and if you're telling us the truth and your daughter is really expecting Sam's baby then I think perhaps we can help."

He frowned. "Eileen, what are you saying?"

"Frank, this could be the answer to our prayers. A baby, Sam's baby. Our niece or nephew. Think about it."

Rose sat quietly watching the couple. Eileen seemed to be silently begging her husband.

"Think about it Frank."

Eventually Frank nodded and Eileen turned back to Karen, beaming.

"Mrs?"

"Barnes."

"Mrs Barnes, my husband and I would like to adopt your daughter's child."

Karen gasped, "really?"

"Yes. The child is our flesh and blood and we haven't been blessed with a baby of our own, although we've been married for eight years. We'd be very loving parents, I promise you."

"I don't doubt that."

"Please, Mrs Barnes, say yes."

"Well I was going to arrange for Karen to stay with my mother in Clapham until the baby's born. I was hoping that I could persuade her to leave the baby at the hospital for adoption and then return home with no-one round our way any the wiser as it were." The woman looked into her husband's face, beaming.

"That would be perfect then. We can have the papers drawn up and be there at the hospital to collect the baby as soon as it's born. She's a minor so you can sign for her can't you?"

"Yes. I suppose I can," Rose replied nodding slowly as she realized there was a way out for her daughter and her family.

Frank stood up and began pacing. After a minute or two he turned. "I must insist that your daughter never try to find the child. I mean ever. If we adopt Sam's baby then he becomes ours. Forever, no going back. Do I make myself clear?" Rose nodded solemnly. "Absolutely, Mr Murphy. I want Karen to live her life as if this never happened. To be able to put it behind her. I promise you, she'll never come knocking. Consider this baby yours."

* * *

2011

Sally opened Rick's front door and called out. Silence. Walking through the house she listened intently. Eventually, as she proceeded upstairs she heard the familiar light snoring of both Rick and Josh.

Josh's door was open; he had crashed out on the bed fully clothed. As she crept in to check on him, in the half-light she saw the blood and bruising on his face and gasped. Then she spotted the empty vodka bottle next to the bed and felt tears fill her eyes.

He stirred and rolled over to grab a pillow and pull it into a pseudo embrace and as she watched him she saw the tears fall from his eyes as he dreamt.

Reversing out the room onto the landing she made her way to Rick's room and saw him tossing restlessly in his sleep. His hair was a mess and the bed was completely disheveled.

She undressed and slipped in beside him. "Mmm," he groaned.

"It's ok hun, it's only me, I just got in from work. Let's have a cuddle then." As he sleepily put his arms around her he opened his eyes and smiled at her lecherously. "Good morning." She giggled.

"Good morning to you."

"Hang on a sec babe, give me ten," and he sprung from the bed into the en-suite and as she waited she heard the toilet flush and the sound of him brushing his teeth.

As he approached the bed he smelt lovely and looked alert and awake. "Fresh as a daisy and all ready for you."

"Come here," she breathed smiling.

He lifted the quilt and climbed underneath. He smelt the shower-gel and shampoo she'd used before leaving work and the toothpaste on her breath. He knew she was exhausted, despite her sexual enthusiasm she looked shattered. Round the eyes, where she couldn't hide it. "You tired hun?" He asked as he pushed a strand of hair behind her ear. "Bit."

"Wanna sleep first?"

"No. I want you first, then sleep, then talk, then you again. That sound ok?"

"Mmm yeah that works for me." they grinned at each other. Taking his hand she ran her thumb over his palm tenderly.

"I looked in on Josh; he looks terrible." Putting a finger to her lips he shook his head.

"Shush. You know the rules. This is just you and me, right here, right now. Everything else gets left outside the door. Make love first, talk later. And FYI, you just lay back and let me do all the work ok, then you can just drift off to sleep."

Stretching her hands above her head she smiled as she kicked off the quilt. "Works for me. Do your stuff, Murphy, I'm all yours."

He smiled down at her as he took her breasts and gently thumbed her hardening nipples.

Leaning down, he took first one then the other in his mouth and worked the nipples with his tongue, both of them enjoying the sensation. As he began to suck and pull she let out a low moan.

Slowly he ran his tongue the length of her stomach, stopping only to tickle her naval. She giggled.

As he approached her tuft he ran his fingers gently through the hair, tickling and caressing. Again she giggled appreciatively.

Silently he placed his palms against the inside of her thighs and eased them apart.

His first glimpse of her pussy always made him smile, feeling his hard-on throbbing he ran a thumb the length of her glistening inner lips and watched as she shivered.

Sliding down the bed he placed his face between her legs and leant forward to kiss her delicate folds as if he were kissing her mouth, his tongue reaching forward to ease into her as he pressed his lips against hers. She was already wet and he was, as ever amazed at the heat inside her. As a nurse he'd seen innumerable women's bodies, he'd washed them, he'd dressed them, he'd administered rectal and vaginal medication to both young and old, and as a student nurse he'd helped deliver babies. None of these experiences ever struck him as anything vaguely sexual. He was a healthcare practitioner and that was that, and as a professional he felt he was fairly experienced and au fait with the female anatomy but whenever he saw Sal's pussy he just lost the plot and wanted nothing more than to dive in and make her come. Hard. Nothing and no-one, not Elaine, or anyone he'd slept with before ever made him feel like that. As he drew back to look at her it occurred to him that there was certain significance in this, and maybe he was feeling something important, something special. Maybe he loved her.

Sliding a finger into her he felt her body respond as she let out another low moan of pleasure. Aware of how tired she must be he took her clitoris in his mouth and began to flick and suck the little nub as he slid another finger inside her and rotated his hand to locate her g-spot. Feeling her hips start to rock as her pussy sucked at his fingers he increased the rhythm to bring her off quickly. As she arched off the bed and thrust her hips into the air he watched her come. She was amazing.

Opening her eyes she looked at him and nodded. "Fuck me. Now."

Smiling he approached her and as he held her hands above her head and sucked at her nipples she reached for his cock but found him soft and flaccid.

"Babe, you ok?" she asked, her eyes full of concern.

"I'm just a little stressed I think, hang on, give me a minute."

Taking his penis in his hand he began to work the shaft, his eyes closed and his brow furrowed. After several minutes he appeared semi-hard but as soon as he stopped his hard-on disappeared.

She took his face in her hands and kissed him hard on the lips. "Please stop. That was lovely when you went down on me and I'm perfectly satisfied and chilled so please stop pumping your poor piston and snuggle up. I'm not surprised you're stressed sweetheart. Who wouldn't be?"

He hung his head, "You sure, Sal? I feel really bad. I'm sorry; I don't know what's wrong with me. I loved making you come but I guess everything's just gotten on top of me lately."

"Shush. Give us a cuddle you."

Eventually her breathing slowed and her face took on the familiar expression of sleep. Looking at her he whispered "I love you."

"I'm not asleep."

"What?"

"I heard you. I was almost asleep. You love me?"

"You were supposed to be asleep. Maybe you misheard?" He teased with a grin.

"Yeah and maybe you love me?"

"Ok. I do."

"Me too. Love you I mean."

"That's a good job then, that could have been embarrass-ing."

She yawned.

"Mmm," as she drifted off to sleep again.

* * *

Throwing some clothes into her overnight bag Lucy wiped the tears from her face for the umpteenth time.

She'd text Kirsty and was waiting for a reply.

She'd decided to stay away for the agreed forty-eight hours then she'd come home and deal with the fall-out.

Her mobile chirped. It was her sister. *That's kwl c u wen u get here.*

CHAPTER 20

Josh opened his eyes and for a split second felt no pain. Then, like a destructive tornado, reality whirled into his consciousness and he felt the familiar grip of heartbreak.

His chest heaved with a dry sob.

His head and hand were both throbbing and his face felt puffy and sore. He reached up and felt the dried blood and studied his fist. He had full movement but some nasty cuts and bruises. He'd have to call Mimi to apologize. He'd been a total bastard. That was totally unacceptable. They had an agreement. She was a prostitute that worked some of the clubs he stood door for and he put work her way and made sure she stayed safe. Occasionally he'd called on her for a little rough stuff when the mood took him. Despite her career choice she'd become a good friend and her reputation for rough, brutal, sex meant she'd been the ideal person to go to. In fact the only person to go to.

The bottle was empty and he cursed. Laying back down he became aware of the soft moans coming from across the landing.

"For fuck's sake," he growled as he buried his head under the pillow.

Unable to lose himself again to sleep he rolled out of bed, kicked his door shut and made his way into the shower.

* * *

As Kirsty opened the door and saw her sister's distressed tear-stained face she gasped.

"Oh my God, what's wrong? Come here." She welcomed Lucy into her arms and held her as she sobbed.

As Lucy quietened she led her into the lounge, sat her down and waited.

Eventually Lucy raised her head and met her sister's eyes. "Something terrible has happened."

Kirsty nodded. "Ok. Go on. Oh shit, is it Mum is she ok? Did the hospital give her bad news...Just tell me, Luce, for Christ's sake what is it?"

"I don't know how to begin. It's almost too much to get my head around."

Again Kirsty nodded. "Luce, please just tell me." Her voice rising with anxiety.

Trying to calm herself Lucy took a deep breath. "You know I've been seeing a lad called Josh?"

"Yeah." Kirsty felt her heart leap in her chest as she remembered the horrific miscarriage and heartbreak Lucy had been through after Tom.

"Well, it's almost impossible to believe but, Mum; our mother. She had a baby when she was fifteen."

Kirsty stood up, shocked "What the fuck? You're joking. No way. How could you know that? And what's that got to do with you and Josh?"

"Oh trust me. She did."

Kirsty shook her head vehemently. "Shit. No, that's not possible."

"Oh babe, it gets worse. Turns out Josh is her grandson, our half nephew."

Kirsty's face paled as she sunk back down into the chair, shocked and shaking. "So that means....Oh shit, oh my God, Luce....You were sleeping with..."

"Yeah. I know." Again the tears ran down her cheeks unhindered.

"Oh hun, that's gross. Shit, not gross...I mean, oh hun, that's terrible. I don't know what to say."

Collapsing into her sister's arms Lucy sobbed. "I love him, I love him so much. He was crying when we found out. He was the one. I know it. What am I gonna do?"

Kirsty literally felt her blood run cold at the thought of her sister's incestuous relationship. "Does Mum know you know? Does she know about Josh? That he's her grandson, and about you and him? Does our Dad know? Shit what a mess."

Lucy lifted her head and wiped her face with the back of her hand.

"She knows I know. She knows about Josh and her son and about me and Josh. I've given her forty-eight hours to tell Dad or I will. As far as she's concerned we can all carry on as normal. She has no intention of acknowledging her son or his family."

Kirsty stood up and stepped away from the sofa as if she could distance herself from the situation. "Fucking hell. Does she really think that's gonna happen?...Tell me, what's our brother like? What's his name?"

Lucy smiled. "His name is Richard Murphy, Rick; he's a charge nurse at St Georges. He's lovely."

"Well Mum can piss off. She can't force us to ignore each other now we know he exists. If I have a brother then I wanna meet him."

Lucy smiled. "You'll like him."

"We all have the right to be a part of each other's lives."

"Kirst' you don't understand, I can't be a part of Rick's life because of Josh. He lives with his Dad and they're really close. I can't go there again and pretend everything's ok...I just can't." Again she burst into tears.

* * *

Mimi's mobile chirped. It was Josh. *cn I pop round plz need to talk?*

She checked the time and text back. *Ok c u in 10.*

Am outside!

She smiled as she walked to the window and saw him standing by his car looking sheepish.

Lol get in here numbnuts, she text back.

She saw him read the message and smile.

Opening the front door she walked ahead of him into the kitchen and put the kettle on.

He followed and stood in the door-way, looking at the floor, obviously embarrassed.

"Mimi...About last night...I'm so sorry for what I said. I didn't mean it."

"I should fucking think so arsehole. It's a good job we're mates and I know you were just being a twat otherwise I might be a tad pissed off."

Looking up he saw her face and the broad grin spread across it and he sighed with relief.

"So...We're ok then? We're good?"

"Course we're good. It's me; you'd have to go a long way to piss me off hun. I get fucked for a living; my bar is set very high. Trust me."

They hugged and she allowed her eyes to close as she felt the tears threaten.

"Thank fuck. You making tea then girl or am I?"

"I'll make it, you sit. Here stick this on your hand," she said handing him a bag of frozen peas, "you look like shit and I'm all ears. Give."

He slumped into a chair and let his head fall backwards and as she made the tea he told her.

* * *

Sally woke to see a hot cup of coffee on the bedside table. "Mmm lovely."

"Yes you are."

Rolling over she saw Rick stretched out beside her fully dressed. "Thanks, what's the time?"

"Twenty past four." She sat up and reached for the coffee.

"Did you sleep ok?"

"Yes thanks. How's Josh?"

"He went out ages ago. Did you see him? He looks like he's had a fight. Poor sod. I feel so sorry for him. This is all my fault. What a fucking mess. I can't believe my life has been turned so completely upside down in the last few weeks."

"Oh hun, no, don't go there, that way lies madness. You didn't know what was in that letter, or about the adoption, or about Josh and Lucy. None of this is your fault?"

"I feel what I feel, and that's guilt."

"Oh, babe, you got nothing to feel guilty about."

"Doesn't stop it though."
She reached over and held him as he wept.

CHAPTER 21

As Rick, Sally and Franny settled in the conservatory he struggled to get his thoughts into some sort of order.

The women waited patiently as he rotated his shoulders and rubbed the back of his neck. Sally took his hand reassuringly. Eventually he looked at his aunt and began.

"I found her."

"Oh my goodness."

"Yes, you could say that."

"Have you spoken to her?"

"Yes."

"And?"

"Oh shit, Franny," he stood up and started pacing. "It's complicated. She got my letter, posted a reply and then got admitted to my ward. She was going to theatre and obviously wanted to tell me who she was before she went, in case something happened I guess. Anyway, she doesn't want anything to do with me or any of the family. Apparently her husband doesn't even know."

"Oh what a shame, I'm so sorry. Do you feel a bit more at peace with it now?" he spun round to face her again.

"Hang on, there's more. It turns out that the Josh had been seeing her daughter, my half-sister."

His aunt's face paled. "What? Really? Seeing as in dating? Oh dear God."

"Yes and it *wasn't* platonic, if you get what I mean. Turns out it was serious too. They're both heart-broken and pretty screwed up. Can you imagine being told you've slept with your aunt?"

Franny frowned and shook her head. She was pale and shocked. "Oh no, that's horrible. Poor Josh." Franny's hand flew to her mouth. It was shaking.

Rick shook his head. "I just wish I'd never opened that bloody letter. What a mess."

"I'm sorry, Richard; perhaps I should have burnt it. I feel partly responsible." His aunt's voice cracked as she struggled with her tears.

"No please don't feel guilty; you had no way of knowing. It's Karen's fault for not telling her husband and kids. If she'd have been honest...Well it wouldn't have stopped Josh and Lucy meeting but it would have meant she and I could've had a relationship of sorts."

"Rick, tell Franny about your father," Sally urged gently. Taking a deep breath he sat down to gather his thoughts.

"She wrote me a letter but I didn't get it until after we'd met. She figured out who I was when she saw me at work the day of her op. Anyway she gave me some info about my Dad in the letter. His name is, get this for a coincidence, Sam Murphy and he was supposed to meet Karen so they could run away together. Apparently, he never showed. She went on to spend the rest of the pregnancy with her grandmother, had me adopted and returned to her life, reputation intact. Maybe he saw what a witch she was and changed his mind. A lucky escape if you ask me. I'm about to start trawling the internet to try and find him." He looked across at his aunt. Her face was ashen. "Franny?...Franny are you ok?"

"Richard, I think I know who your Sam was," she whispered.

"What?"

"Your Dad had a younger brother named Sam. He was killed one night, hit by a car in the fog, it was November 1967. Apparently he had a suitcase, all his money and a transfer letter from the bank he worked at for a new job in Kent. No-one knew why he was leaving but I suppose it's feasible that he was running away with your mother and he was killed on the way to meet her."

"Jesus, that sounds too much of a coincidence doesn't it? Shit, is it possible he didn't let her down?"

"Maybe not."

"So your parents adopted their nephew then?" Sally mused. "How the hell did that happen? That's weird. There's a lot more going on here I reckon."

Franny studied Rick's face. "It would appear so. That explains why you looked like Frank. Frank and Sam were the image of each other."

* * *

She sat silently as Josh poured out his heart.

Once he'd finished she stood up and walked round to him and put her arms around his neck.

"What a fucking mess huh?" He whispered.

"Jesus, no wonder you were in such a state. You wanna go upstairs?"

He sighed. "Erm...Tempting as that is I really can't, Mimi. It's too soon after Lucy. What happened last night, that was anger. I wanted to hurt and *be* hurt. Sorry. You do understand don't you?"

Her heart took a dive. She'd completely misread the situation. What she'd taken as a chance to have a relationship, turned out to be just another angry punter. Turning away from him she busied herself with wiping the worktops. "That's fine mate, just thought I'd offer."

"Mimi...Mimi." She turned and he saw the pain in her eyes. "Shit," he muttered. Taking her in his arms he held her until she eventually stopped resisting and leant into his body. "Babe, I'm sorry, I didn't mean to give you the wrong idea."

"What are you talking about?"

"Maybe I'm wrong, but I got the impression I just hurt your feelings when I said no thanks."

She pushed him away with an air of bravado. "What? Oh, Josh, you flatter yourself hun. You know me, fucking seriously disturbed individuals is my job. The angry, the aggressive, the seriously warped. That's my stock in trade. Just letting you know you are welcome to another arse kicking anytime. On the house." He smiled.

"Does that tough image actually fool anyone?"

"Fuck off."

"No, seriously. Does it? Cause I see right through you girl. You might sleep with some twisted fucks for a living but I don't believe for one moment that's who you are." She spun round to face him, her face alive with fury.

"Where do you get off telling me who I am? You don't know me. Not really. What you see is all there is. I am a whore. I am a dominatrix, I am a sex-slave, I am a commodity. My cunt is my meal-ticket. Simple as. Used and abused as needed. Didn't hear you complaining about my career choice as you drove your cock into me last night you fucking hypocrite."

Silently Josh stared at her. "Well? Nothing to say now?" She challenged. He shook his head. "No. I thought not. Just like the others aren't you?" He sighed as he reached for his tea.

"If you say so then I guess I am," he smirked.

She sat down opposite him and shook her head. "Don't agree with me you stupid bastard."

"Ok then, I'm not. Happy?" She laughed as he continued, "I'm not gonna fight with you whatever you say. You might be a professional sex-worker but you're a good friend and I care about you. If I could change what happened last night I would but quite frankly I didn't know where else to go. Mimi, I hate what you do but I respect you for doing it if that makes sense?"

"You knob," she teased. "I'm a whore. If I can live with it why can't you?"

"Simple. I care more about you than you do. Live with it."

* * *

Jack sat next to her and took hand. She continued to stare at the television. "Sweetheart?"

"Mmm?"

"You ok?"

"Yes fine thanks. Why?"

He reached over and switched the TV to standby. "Because something happened between you and Lucy and I want to know what it is and I want to know now. That rubbish about my birthday was obviously a load of ole flannel and now I want the truth." Her heart jumped.

"We had words that's all. It's nothing."

"You come home from hospital and she moves in with Kirsty. That's not only completely out of character for her that's impossible to believe. Furthermore, Kirsty hasn't been to see you since you came home. Again, totally unlike her. You're gonna tell me, or they will."

She felt her heart start to pound in her chest as she struggled for breath. "Jack...Help me...I can't breathe... Please." Un-fazed he took her calmly by the shoulders and talked her through the anxiety.

"It's a panic attack, just put your hands over your mouth and slow your breathing down. That's it. Nice and slow." Eventually she calmed down as her breathing returned to normal. "Oh love that was horrible. I couldn't breathe. I was so scared."

"I know, panic attacks are scary but you're ok now. Just relax. Then when you're ready you can tell me what's going on."

"No, Jack. No. Please I can't. I just can't. It's private."

"I'm not having that. You bloody well tell me what's going on or I'm going to Kirsty's right now and I'll tell you this, those girls will damn well tell me. Either way this ends now. Ok?"

She nodded once as she felt the tears threaten. She briefly contemplated concocting a lie to fit her story but she knew the girls wouldn't back her up. Suddenly realizing there was no way out she took her husband's hands in hers, took a deep breath and began.

* * *

Logging on to the registrar's web-site he began to fill in the search criteria for Sam Murphy. The death certificate would take at least five working days to arrive but it felt like he was a step closer to his father.

He spun the chair round to face her. "All done?" She asked.

"Yep. I have the address of the churchyard. Franny's told me where the grave is. Apparently it's in the next row from your Mum and Dad's, well, Frank and Eileen's, oh you know what I mean." She smiled and reached up to kiss him.

"Shall we go then?"

He hesitated and finally nodded. "Ok."

"Sure?" She took his hand. It was shaking.

"Yeah. I need to do this." His voice cracked with emotion.

He collected the flowers from the kitchen sink and shaking the excess water off he placed them in a plastic bag. "They're beautiful," she mused.

"Am I being a bit soppy taking flowers, Sal?"

"Oh hun, no way. It's lovely."

"Really?"

"Absolutely."

CHAPTER 22

Her hands were shaking uncontrollably. "When I was fifteen I was in love with a chap four years older than me." She paused as he nodded to encourage her, his smile full of reassurance. "Unfortunately I ended up in the family-way..."

"What?" He pulled his hands from hers, his eyes wide with shock.

"Please, Jack, just listen. Let me finish. If you're gonna hear this then you're gonna have to hear it all in one go."

"But...You just said..." His face was contorted with confusion and sorrow. "You were pregnant?"

"Yes. I know how this sounds but please let me carry on."

"Sorry." He muttered, struggling to hold his temper as she took another deep breath.

"We were supposed to run away together but he never turned up. When I told my Mum she arranged for me to go and stop with Aunty Olive and Nan until the baby was born. I never got to see it or hold it...It, he, was taken by the adoptive parents. I went home with my reputation intact. Then I met you and knew I had a chance to be happy...I lied to you, Jack I'm so very sorry but I just wanted to pretend none of it had happened." She sobbed as she reached for his hands. His face was pale and his eyes reflected shock and disappointment. "You had another man's baby and you never told me?"

"Yes. I'm sorry."

"You're sorry?"

"Yes..." She reached for his arm.

"YOU'RE SORRY?" He shouted pulling away.

"Jack please," she implored.

"When we got together you played the little innocent so well. 'Ooh, Jack, you're my first, ooh, Jack, be gentle,'" he mimicked. "What a fucking idiot I am."

"It wasn't like that. I loved you. I still do."

"But not enough to tell the truth eh?" He stood up and began pacing the room.

"Telling anyone wasn't an option. Mum told me if I wanted to put it behind me I wasn't to tell anybody. Not even you. I had no choice. Do you have any idea what it was like for me to be alone and pregnant at fifteen? I was thrown a lifeline and I took it."

He stopped and stared at her. "Is that what I was to you? A lifeline? A way out?"

"No. It wasn't like that. Please try to understand." He stood silently looking out of the window with his back to her clenching and unclenching his fists. She stood and placed her hand between his shoulder blades. "Get the fuck away from me," he snarled. She jumped back.

Sitting back down she continued, her voice cracking with emotion. "My baby...My son only found out he was adopted recently when the adoptive mother died. He wrote to me..."

Jack spun to face her. "That letter? It was for you wasn't it? You were the Karen Barnes he was looking for?" She nodded.

"Yes. It was me. He found me too." She paused and raised her eyes to meet his gaze. "It's the nurse from ward seventeen."

"Rick?"

"Yes."

"Rick Murphy. The Rick Murphy I know, is your son?"

"Yes."

Looking deflated Jack slumped onto the floor by the window and hung his head in his hands.

Tentatively she continued. "I told him I didn't want him in my life. I didn't want you or the girls upset. I told him to back off but it was too late."

"Too late?"

"They'd met by then."

"Who?" He looked up.

Her voice wavered. "Lucy and Rick's son. My grandson. Lucy's been seeing Rick's son Josh. That's how she found out."

"WHAT THE FUCK?" He screamed, "you're telling me Lucy is sleeping with her...What? Her...Nephew?"

"Yes," she whispered.

"Shit! What a fucking mess. Let me get this straight. You lied to me for over thirty years. Rejected your own son. And your daughter ended up in an incestuous relationship."

Reaching out for him she pleaded, "I know how bad it is Jack. Believe me."

"Do you really? Well it's about to get a lot worse. I want you out of this house," he snarled, glaring at her.

"What?" Her face contorted with shock and incomprehension.

"Out. Today. It's over, Karen. I can't believe you kept this from me for all these years."

"Jack, please," she implored, a hand reaching for him.

He turned his head away. "You move your stuff out or I will. Simple. I'm going over to Kirsty's. Be gone by the time I get back." He stood and turned his back to her again.

"Jack, I love you. Where am I supposed to go?" She whimpered.

"You could try and find your ex, maybe he'll take you in eh?" Bitterness coloring every word.

She stood to intercept him as he made for the door but as she stepped forward she felt his hand strike her cheek. "You bitch! Don't ever try to touch me again, do you understand?"

* * *

The doorbell rang and as Alex opened the door Jack collapsed into the hall. "KIRST! LUCE! QUICK HELP ME!"

"Oh my God Dad? Are you ok?" Lucy fell to her knees and cradled her father's head in her arms. Huge sobs wracked his body. Kirsty struggled to get close to her Dad and as she took his hands in hers he crumpled even further into their embrace. A broken man.

Eventually Jack was calm enough to stand with a little help from Alex and his daughters led him into the lounge.

Staring at the carpet he slowly began to speak, his voice was hoarse from crying as he struggled to verbalize his feelings. "It's over. I...I told her to be gone by the...The time I get back." He stuttered. His voice thick with emotion.

"Dad no. Surely you don't mean that?" Kirsty asked, clearly shocked. Her gaze meeting Alex's as he questioned her with his eyes. She shrugged in response, unable to comprehend her father's words and having no answer for him. "Mum made a mistake, that's all. Can't you forgive her?" she ventured. Instantly Lucy jumped to her father's defense, her anger evident. "Kirsty are you mad? A mistake? It's a bit more than that. She lied to him, to all of us. She kept this from Dad every day they were together. It's not a simple mistake. She has a son. We have a brother. What about me and Josh?" Her eyes filled with tears. "Do you know how that feels? We slept together. We fell in love and he's my nephew. I can't see a way to deal with that at the moment. It hurts too much and it's all her fault." Alex reached out and put a calming hand on his wife's arm. She stopped and took a deep breath.

"Yes I know all that. But she's our mother. She's his wife, that must count for something?"

"ENOUGH!" Jack shouted, jumping to his feet. "I don't know what's going to happen but I know I can't be around her at the moment so it's better if she moves out at least for a bit. That's it. I need some space. No more discussion."

Part 2

CHAPTER 23

She emerged from the club with a group of young men. All well-dressed but obviously drunk. She was dressed provocatively and one of the men attempted to pull her basque down. She playfully slapped his hand away as she tried to stop another from thrusting his hand up her short skirt. "Hey boys, time and place, time and place. Let's get in the car and we can play in private huh?" She urged.

Josh opened the limo's back door as the group stumbled in. He raised his eyebrows to ask if she was ok. She nodded. The other girl due to accompany Mimi had called in sick and apparently no-one else had been able to fill in at short notice.

As he pulled out into the city traffic he lowered the partition and caught a glimpse of Mimi on her back, her breasts exposed, being sucked and mauled by two different guys as another was forcing his cock into her mouth. She appeared in control but the image made his breath catch in his throat.

The group then started chanting, and as the stag came all over Mimi's face, they cheered. Within seconds the next had rammed his penis into her mouth as another ripped her thong off.

A horn blared as Josh narrowly missed a bus. "Shit." As he slammed on the brakes the group hurled abuse at him before continuing. Her face was obscured by thrusting buttocks but it appeared as if she was sucking one penis whilst two other guys rammed into her vaginally and anally. For a second he thought he heard her scream. Barely glancing at the road he turned to look over his shoulder. "Mimi, Mimi. You ok?"

"Fuck off and drive." Growled a male voice.

"I'm talking to her, not you. Mimi, answer me." He persisted.

"She knows better than to talk with her mouth full." The crowd hooted and cheered. The guy nearest to Josh turned towards the front of the car. "Mind your own fucking business shit-head or I'll have your job and your fucking license." The partition rose leaving him in silence.

Josh slammed his hand on the steering wheel. He knew that theoretically she *should* be able to handle this crowd, that she *should* be in control, but still, it felt wrong and he wanted to drag each and every one of them out of the car and kick the shit out of them. Something about this crowd bothered him. Pushing his worries to the back of his mind he imagined they were just the usual stag party, pissed up and acting rough. Nothing to really worry about. Mimi would have called out if there was a problem.

After half an hour he pulled up outside the private club she usually worked at and opened the back door. The men spilled out onto the damp grey pavement and wandered drunkenly into the club.

Peering into the limo he saw her on the floor. Virtually naked. Bruised and bleeding. Her eyes were swollen and blackening, her lip was split, her breasts bruised, she had blood on her thighs and buttocks and she appeared unconscious. "MIMI! Shit. Oh God Babe. Open your eyes hun." Taking off his jacket he wrapped her up before lifting her onto the seat. Her eyes flickered.

* * *

Karen stood staring at the familiar front door, her suitcase sitting beside her. She sighed as she lifted her hand to ring the bell. She was weak from her surgery and she knew carrying the case hadn't helped. The door opened on the chain and a wrinkled face appeared.

"Blimey. It's you. What you doing here?" Her mother asked.

"Can I come in please, Mum?" The door closed as the chain was unhitched.

"I suppose. What's with the suitcase? Something you need to tell me?"

"Please, Mum, can we just do this indoors?"

"Suit yourself," and the old woman shuffled away down the narrow hallway.

Karen closed the door behind her. The case had made her hand sore and she eased it tenderly before following her mother into the living room.

"Chucked you out has he?" She chuckled. Karen refused to reply. "Well?"

"Why are you asking when you know the answer?"

Her mother scowled at her. "Really? Didn't think he had it in him. What happened? Come on, spit it out. Don't tell me you've been messing around with someone else?"

"Any chance of a cup of tea first please?"

"I'm not your bloody slave. You know where the kitchen is."

Wearily Karen made two cups of tea and returned to the dreary room to face the inevitable. Taking a deep breath she lifted her head to meet her mother's gaze. Those small, sparkling, eyes; hard as flint.

"My son found me."

Rose coughed as she struggled not to choke on her tea. "What did you say?"

"My son. My baby, well he's forty-three now, but I'm sure you know that. Well his adoptive parents died and they left a letter telling him all about me and he found me."

"Bloody hell!" Her voice softened. "What's he like?"

"He's the image of his Dad. He seemed like a nice chap I suppose."

"Does he know about the girls, that you're married, about me?"

"Yes, he knows, but it gets worse, a lot worse actually. It turns out that he works at the same hospital with Jack so they know each other which is difficult enough but our Lucy had been getting serious with his son. In other words, my grandson, and she's heartbroken not to mention the whole incest issue." Rose slammed her cup and saucer down.

"Jesus Christ, Ka. What a bleeding mess."

"I tried to contain it, Mum I really did," she whispered, "I told him not to contact me again, that I wouldn't have Jack and the girls hurt but once Lucy found out she threatened to tell Jack." Karen hung her head in her hands.

"So you told him?"

"I had to." She mumbled.

"Yes I suppose you did. I'm sorry it's come to this I am really, but you've done well to keep it secret all these years."

Karen's head drooped further as her voice cracked. "I've lost everything. Everyone I love hates me. Jack's chucked me out. Oh, Mum..." Struggling to rise, the older woman passed her daughter a tissue and patted her arm. "Give 'em all time, love. It's a shock. That whole Lucy business, well that'll take a bit to come back from but just give 'em a chance to get their heads round it all."

Karen sipped her tea and wandered to the window. Looking out onto the little balcony and the city lights twenty floors below she felt as chill run through her. "Mum?"

"Mmm?"

"That night you went out and came back and told me it was all arranged. The adoption and everything. Where did you go?"

"Where do you think? I went to find the toe rag responsible for getting my girl into trouble."

"WHAT?" She spun to face her mother.

"That Sam. I went to his house." Karen slumped back down onto the tatty sofa, her mouth hanging open.

"What did he say?"

"What? What do you mean?..." The old woman frowned and peered at her daughter. "Oh Christ, you don't know do you? After all these years I thought you'd have found out somehow. Tried to find him maybe. Traced his family. I'm sorry love. He's dead. He was killed on the way to meet you. He was hit by a car in the fog."

Karen stared at her mother, too stunned to respond. As her body started shaking she felt the bile rise in her throat as she rushed for the bathroom.

"Ka, KA! You alright love?"

She returned wiping her mouth on a piece of toilet paper. She was ashen.

"Dead. Sam was killed. Oh God, so he didn't let me down, he was coming to meet me. He did love me."

"Maybe he did. His family said he had all his clothes packed, money. Even a letter saying he had a new job."

Karen sobbed as fresh tears fell. "His family?"

"Yes, I spoke to them. It was his brother and sister-in-law who told me what had happened."

"Frank and Eileen."

"Yes," she nodded. "Did you ever meet them?"

"No, but Sam mentioned them all the time. He lived with them." Rose struggled to her feet and made her way to the sofa. Sitting down she placed her arm around her daughter's shoulders. Karen crumpled into the embrace. "Well darlin' they adopted your baby. We arranged it between us. They adopted their nephew."

Karen lifted her head and smiled. "Really? That explains the same surname then. But why didn't you ever tell me?"

"If you'd have known wouldn't you have wanted to go to Sam's funeral? To see your baby? To get in touch? I couldn't let that happen. You had a chance to walk away from this without anyone ever knowing what you'd done. If you could convince Jack you were a virgin who'd had an unfortunate accident as a littl'un then you were home and dry. I did it for all of us. It would have brought such shame to the family to have you in the family-way especially at that age. Blimey girl what was I supposed to do? I did what I thought was right and your Dad agreed. What better parents could there be for your baby than his own flesh and blood?"

* * *

As Michelle's eyes rolled back in her head Josh hit the third nine on his phone key pad.

"Hang on hun, they'll be here soon." His hands shook as he struggled to get her into the recovery position.

A face appeared at the open doorway. "You'll have to move it mate, got other cars waiting to drop off."

"Eddie, mate, give us a minute. She's unconscious; the ambulance is on its way. They'll have to wait," Josh snapped. The man peered at the back seat. "Shit isn't that Mimi? One of our girls?"

"Yep, a bunch of arseholes beat the shit out of her for a stag night jolly and pissed off inside to carry on the fun."

The doorman frowned. "They're in here?" He asked as he gestured towards the entrance behind him.

"Yep."

"Get her sorted, move the car and we'll have a private word with them. You and me. You up for that my friend?"

As the sirens approached Josh grinned humorlessly. "Fuck yeh."

* * *

As the ambulance pulled away Josh headed for the club. Eddie met his gaze and nodded almost imperceptibly.

The blaring music and dim lighting made it difficult to identify the group but as the two men split up they soon found the stag party heading for a private room with several girls.

The doorman took the lead and as he approached the stag he took his arm in a vice-like grip. "Excuse me sir, would you like to step into the office with me please? There's a problem with your membership."

"Fuck off!" He replied as he tried to pull away.

Eddie tightened his grip on one arm as Josh took the other. "Oy you bastards, fuck off!" He struggled furiously as the rest of the party, suddenly alerted to their mate's problem, began to respond noisily.

Josh gripped the man's arm hard and put his mouth to his ear. "Tell 'em to back off or I'll drop you where you stand you piece of shit. Get me?"

He grinned reassuringly at the others as he responded through gritted teeth. "It's ok guys, really, it's just a bit of business that's all. I'll be right back." The other men stopped and studied the huge doormen and the seriously drunk stag, still unhappy to leave the groom-to-be, in what appeared to be a risky situation. "I'll come with you mate," one guy called.

"NO! No really, it's fine, Stu, honest," he protested but his friend left the crowd to stand with them. "Come on then, where's this fucking paperwork you arseholes? We've got some serious drinking to get on with." The group cheered as Josh and Eddie led the men towards the fire exit.

CHAPTER 24

"Have you heard from her?" Kirsty asked tentatively.

"No, why should I?"

"'Cause she's our Mum."

"Have *you* then?"

"Yep."

"And?"

"And what?"

"Is she ok?"

"Like you care."

"Where's she stopping?"

"Why are you asking me when you could easily text her yourself. You know where she is."

"At Nan's?"

"Yep."

"Kirst' I just can't forgive her that's all. I still worry about her. I still want to know she's ok but I don't wanna see her or speak to her. Have you seen her?"

"No but I'm taking the twins over tomorrow. Wanna come?"

"Definitely not, thanks."

"Can I send her your love?"

"No you bloody can't. You can just tell her I was asking after her. That's all, ok?" Kirsty put her hands up. "Ok, ok. Fine. Whatever."

Lucy poured the water into the cups as her sister sat down. "How's Dad doing?"

"Rough." Lucy placed the cups on the table and sat down opposite her sister. "He's really struggling. I'm so worried."

"They just need time that's all."

"You don't really think they'll get back together do you?"

"They've been together a long time. I hope they can sort themselves out."

"So if Alex suddenly confessed to having a kid with another woman you'd be able to carry on as normal? I don't think so."

"Oh, Lucy, life isn't always black and white. All the years of love Mum and Dad have behind them has to count for something." Reaching for the sugar Kirsty studied her sister's face before continuing. "I was wondering. Have you heard from Rick?"

"Yeah, we've been texting. He asked me if we'd both like to meet for lunch sometime. Please say yes."

The sisters both sipped their coffees. "Ok."

"That's brilliant, Kirst'. Thanks."

"I'm not taking sides though. I'm gonna tell Mum and Dad that we're meeting ok?"

"Of course it is. I know he'd really like a relationship with Mum if she'd let him. She's got nothing to hide now so why can't she just talk to him?"

"Again with the whole black and white thing. It's not that simple. Dad's her first priority and that's how it should be. If we're ok with it it's one less thing for her to worry about though so she should be pleased we're getting used to the idea."

"How the hell am I supposed to ever go to Rick's or have a family get together when it means having to face Josh?"

"I know hun…"

Lucy slammed her cup down sending coffee all over the table. "DON'T YOU DARE! Just don't ok. You'll never know. You can never understand how I feel. How much it took to trust him, to allow myself to love someone again and then to find that it's over without either of us being to blame. He wasn't a cheat, he's not married, he loves me but through no fault of my own it's over. Do you know I actually thought about changing my name and being sterilized so that we could still be together without breaking the law or risking having kids?"

Kirsty placed a hand over her sister's. "I'm sorry babe I didn't mean to sound patronizing. It's totally shit and I do know how hurt you are. Really. As to the whole family get-together scenario, well I don't know if Dad would ever be ok with that either so I wouldn't worry too much about it for now. It's just nice to spend time with Rick and get to know him. If you're up for that I'm happy."

"What about his girls, have you met them?"

"No. You?"

"Yeah, I met 'em at the hospital when Rick fell down the stairs. They were really nice. I've met Elaine and Sally, the ex and the girl-friend and they're both lovely too."

"Oh, Luce, please come and see Mum with me. Please," she implored. Lucy stood and moved to the patio doors. Resting her head against the cool glass she closed her eyes. Silently, Kirsty moved over to stand behind her and as her arms slipped around her in a hug Lucy dissolved into tears.

* * *

As the fire-door opened into the alley Josh's foot connected with the back of the man's knee and he went down, face first onto the gravel. "Fuck!" He shouted but before he could stand Josh launched himself onto his back and grabbed him by the throat. The man's hands clutched at Josh's arm as he fought for breath. Josh became vaguely aware of scuffling noises elsewhere in the darkness as his colleague tackled the companion.

He felt the man weaken and as his fight abated Josh released his throat and slammed his face into the dirt before flipping him over and landing a sharp kick to the belly. The man groaned, his face bloody, his nose clearly broken. He gasped for breath as he tried to aim a kick at Josh's knee cap. He was too slow and Josh moved back easily.

"Enough...Fuck this...I've had enough," he groaned, struggling to his feet.

Josh leant down to stare into the man's face. "You fucking cunt. I say when you've had enough. Not you."

As the man struggled onto all fours Josh's kick landed him squarely in the face and he fell backwards almost in slow motion, landing unconscious in a puddle.

Josh turned to see the Eddie standing over his victim who also appeared to be bloody and unconscious in the dim light.

The two victors grinned self-consciously. "That felt fucking good. What are we gonna do with 'em?"

The doorman shrugged. "Don't give a fuck. Leave 'em here."

"Works for me," Josh agreed. Eddie activated his radio.

"Steve, I'll be back in a minute but can you and Pete chuck the rest of that stag party out. Take all their membership cards off 'em and make it clear they're not welcome here anymore ok?"

"You sure you want all the membership cards confiscated? Isn't that what's his name off the tele?"

"I don't give a flying fuck who it is. Get rid ok?"

"Ok. You're the boss."

* * *

Having left the limo parked Josh took a taxi to the nearest hospital and it was only when he was en-route that he realized he had no idea which hospital Mimi had been taken to. They were in the West End and ambulances often went to the hospital with the least amount of patients rather than the nearest. "Shit." He leant forward to speak to the cabbie. "Can you pull over for a minute please?"

"Sure mate."

After trying the three nearest emergency departments he located her and instructed the driver.

* * *

She was pale and bruised and his heart leapt as he saw her. She was connected to a drip and they told him she'd been given some pain relief and was a little drowsy. He stepped inside the curtains and pulled them closed behind him. She opened her eyes as much as she was able and as she saw him she burst into tears. He took her in his arms as best he could and stroked her hair as she sobbed.

The curtains opened and a nurse appeared. "Oh, I'm sorry, Mimi I didn't realize you had a visitor. Are you the next of kin sir?" Before Josh could reply Mimi's croaky voice answered for him. "Yes he is. Tell him everything. It's ok. I give you permission."

The nurse gestured for Josh to sit down.

"Mimi's suffered a particularly violent sexual assault resulting in some nasty internal injuries both in her vagina and her rectum which will need suturing under anesthetic. The attack also, sadly resulted in a miscarriage. We'll take Mimi to theatre shortly and make sure she's not retaining anything of the pregnancy and stitch her wounds at the same time." A sob escaped Mimi's lips as he felt her clutch his hand.

"Oh babe," he whispered as he stroked her hair and reached to kiss her forehead.

"It was yours," she breathed.

"What hun? What did you say?" He leaned closer and put his ear against her swollen lips. She took a deep breath and repeated. "I think it was yours. The baby. That night your Dad told you about Lucy. We didn't use anything and I worked it out from my dates. I got pregnant."

He pulled away abruptly and stared at her. "What the fuck? Mine? Really?" She nodded as he slumped into the chair. "Shit. Why didn't you tell me?"

"Don't you think you had enough going on? You didn't want me and I didn't want you sticking by me out of guilt or pity. Now I'm sorry I didn't tell you." She started crying again. The nurse had slipped out and he climbed onto the trolley next to her and took her in his arms as she cried. Eventually as her sobs abated he spoke softly. "I gave him a kicking."

"Who?"

"The stag, the groom-to-be. The fucking ring-leader. I took him out the back alley and kicked his arse. The head doorman; Eddie, he came with me, it was his idea. He beat up one of the other guys and he got 'em all chucked out and their memberships cancelled." She instantly pushed him away, her face turning scarlet.

"What the fuck? NO! What if they call the police?"

"That's not really very likely is it?" He reasoned.

"But Josh..."

"Shush," he placed a finger on her lips. "It's done but I wish I'd come here first. I'd have killed the cunt."

"I'm glad you didn't. Josh, please don't make this worse. Leave it. For me? You don't know those guys, you don't know who they are."

"I don't need to. They treated you like shit. They hurt you so we hurt them back. Simple as." He kissed her forehead as she wept.

CHAPTER 25

They approached the house nervously. Sensing the stress around them the twins grizzled anxiously. "Shush now. That's enough." Kirsty chided to no avail. As they neared the front door the sisters instinctively reached for each other's hands.

Before they could ring the bell the door was opened by a young woman Lucy recognized from the hospital. She smiled warmly at them both. "Hi, Lucy. Nice to see you again. Hiya, Kirsty. I'm Chloe, come in."

As they battled the double buggy into the hall they were met by Elaine who hugged them both warmly before leading them into the sitting room. She was enthralled by the twins, and they with her and as she released them from their restraints they instantly took her hands and joined her on the floor to play with the toys she'd thoughtfully borrowed for the day.

Amy came in from the kitchen as they sat nervously. "Hi, Lucy."

"Hi, Amy. This is my sister Kirsty. Kirst' this is Amy."

Kirsty smiled. "Hi. Thanks for letting us meet here."

"No probs," Elaine replied. "Would you like tea or coffee? Rick and Sally will be here in a minute. They just stopped off en route to pick up some milk for me. He's a bundle of nerves bless him."

All five women laughed. "I bet. If he's half as nervous as we are he'll be in a right state." Lucy joked.

"I think he's worse," replied Chloe.

"Sally will sort him out. Don't worry." Her mother reassured her.

"I bloody hope so."

Just as they started to relax they heard voices from the kitchen. Both Millson girls exchanged glances. Seeing their anxious looks Elaine stood and opened the kitchen door. "Don't worry; it's just Rick and Sally. They always use the back way. Now was it tea or coffee ladies?" She smiled as she scanned the room.

Rick's face was pale and he clutched Sally's hand so tightly she had to release his fingers to allow the circulation to return. Staying in the kitchen to help Elaine she kissed him on the lips before sending him through the doorway nodding reassuringly.

As he entered the sitting room his daughters rose to greet him with reassuring hugs before slipping into the kitchen discretely.

He stood for several seconds, unsure how to act until he eventually smiled and opened his arms. "Come on then you two. How about a hug for your big brother."

* * *

His mobile bleeped and as he read the text he felt his pulse quicken as he began to panic. *It's Eddie from the club. Have u seen the papers. We need to talk. Tb*

Josh re-read the message. "Shit" he muttered. It was the doorman who'd beaten up the best-man after Michelle's attack. Wondering what the papers had to do with him he made his way to the newsagent.

* * *

Within ten minutes they were chatting as if they'd known each other forever. The twins sat comfortably on Rick's lap and the house was filled with the sound of laughter. They each took turns telling stories about their childhoods and explaining various bumps and scars. By the time the others had returned the atmosphere was relaxed and friendly.

"At the risk of getting all soppy here can I just say thanks to Lucy and Kirsty for coming over today and to Elaine for letting us invade her home? I really appreciate it."

Lucy and Kirsty exchanged smiles and Sally put her arm round his shoulders. "Ok enough with the sentiment. Who wants another bicky?"

* * *

'REALITY SHOW WINNER MUGGED ON STAG-NIGHT' TV show winner Chris Hughes and his best-man Stuart Levins were attacked last night outside a private club in Soho whilst on Hughes' stag-night. The pair became separated from the rest of the group and were viciously mugged and beaten. Their jewelry, wallets and mobile phones were all taken. Hughes who was due to marry former WAG and glamour model Amelia Turner this weekend has had to postpone the ceremony as he will have to undergo extensive surgery to correct a broken nose, fractured cheekbone and have dental implants to replace lost teeth. Both families are said to be incensed by the attack. Police are currently looking for anyone who may have any information. The cost of delaying the wedding is estimated at £30,000.

* * *

Josh's hands shook as he re-read the front page. The bruised and battered face staring out at him was all too familiar. "Fuck." Reaching for his mobile he compiled a text.

CHAPTER 26

"Dad, I need to talk to you,"

"Alright love, fancy a cuppa?"

"No I'm good ta. Look can you just sit down. Please?" Jack looked at his eldest daughter, sighed and took a seat at the table next to her. She took his hand and smiled. "We've been seeing Rick."

"Right."

"And his family."

"And?"

"Well we thought it only fair to tell you. That's all."

He withdrew his hand, stood and made his way slowly over to the kettle. She thought he looked old and tired. "That's very good of you but it's really nothing to do with me is it love? You and your sister, well you're adults and you can see who you want to see. None of my business really." Standing to join him Kirsty put her hand over his and turned her father to face her. "It has everything to do with you. He's our half-brother and that makes you his step-dad. He's Mum's son. He's family. His kids are your step-grand-daughters. You're involved whether you like it or not. Sorry." She withdrew her hand and sat back down, leaving him to think through her words.

Putting his cup on the table he sat down and sighed. "What a fucking mess, Kirst'. I mean what a fucking load of shit this is. One day you're trogging through life and suddenly everything you thought you knew and everyone you thought you had has disappeared. I miss her you know."

She saw his eyes misting up. "I know and she misses you too..."

"WHAT?"

"I said she..."

"I heard what you said. Have you seen her then?"

"Of course. She's still my Mum and the boy's Nana."

"You've actually been to visit her then? Is she with yer Nan?"

"You know she is. Where else would she be?"

"Well, I wasn't sure if she'd found her fancy man, you know, Rick's Dad?"

"Oh for God's sakes will you listen to yourself? She was fifteen. A child. She made a mistake that's all. A huge mistake and now she's alone and miserable and on anti-depressants and you miss each other."

"Anti-depressants? You didn't tell me she was ill"

"Would you have listened?"

"Mmm well, I'm listening now."

"Dad, she's miserable without you and she won't see Rick because of you."

"That's bloody stupid."

"No it's not. She blames him for finding her and for hurting you. She thinks seeing him will make things worse between you."

"It's not his fault, poor bugger. He's just another victim in this mess. I see him at work and we're ok. We're talking to each other."

"She wants to know if you'll see her."

"No."

"No, as in not today? No, as in not at the moment or no as in never?"

He slammed his fist on the table and she visibly jumped. The cup fell and tea streamed across the table. "Oh bollocks!"

Standing and reaching for the cloth she placed a hand on his arm to reassure him. "It's ok, I've got it."

"Thanks, love. Sorry about that, it's just that I miss her but I can't let this go. Every time I think about her and someone else, in bed...Well you know. Her being pregnant too. At fifteen. Would have called her a dirty little slut in my day."

"It was your day, Dad. That's the point. That's exactly why she lied. 'Cause everyone would have called her a slut like you just did. No one would have understood her getting pregnant at fifteen. They'd have judged her just as you have. Don't tell me you never had another girl before Mum?"

Drawing himself up in the chair he looked her in the eye, "Actually, I was a virgin when I met her. I'd had girlfriends and we'd fooled around but I'd never gone all the way." His voice broke with emotion, "She was the first girl I loved and the first I slept with and that's the truth. When she told me I was her first I was so happy I'd waited. I felt that it was meant to be, that we'd saved ourselves for our first true love. What a fucking crock that was," he sighed bitterly.

"Oh Dad, I'm so sorry I didn't know. I just assumed you'd had other lovers."

"Yes well, we weren't like you are today; going out with someone didn't mean shagging them. You might have copped a feel but that was it."

"I didn't realize, Dad. I think I understand how you feel now. No wonder you're so hurt."

Wiping his face with his hands he shrugged and stood. "That's enough of that anyway. I don't want to see her and that's it. Just tell her ok?"

"Are you sure? Can I tell her you miss her?"

"No."

* * *

Eddie was sitting at a corner table nursing a pint. As Josh approached he looked up. "Thanks for coming mate. Drink?"

"Yeh, I'll get 'em. Same again or you want a short?"

"JD'd be nice. Cheers"

Returning to the table with drinks Josh took in the man's hunched shoulders, the way he sat with his back to the door and the furtive way he checked out the room every few minutes.

"Eddie, what's going on?"

"Those cunts we twatted, the ones from the stag do. The two blokes who beat up Mimi..."

"Yeh, I know. They're in the paper."

Eddie took a huge gulp of his drink. "They know who we are."

"So?"

"They know who we are," he repeated. "Word has it that they're coming for us. Both of us and they mean business."

"Oh fuck off. That's just talk. Don't tell me you're scared of those bastards?"

"Fucking right I am. Don't you know who he is? We are in deep shit mate I'm telling you and I'm out of here for a bit. I'm going to work at a club in Manchester and if you've got any sense you'll fuck off out of it too."

Josh shook his head. "Piss off, it's all talk. Trust me. It's bull."

Eddie grabbed his forearm and pushed his face up against Josh's until they were almost nose to nose. "They reckon they're gonna kill us. Postponing that wedding and the cost of all the dental surgery, Hughes reckons we owe him best part of fifty grand and I hear he plans to collect one way or the other."

Josh shrugged off the other man's hand and backed away. "Fuck off," he jeered.

Eddie stood and having checked the bar again he leant down to whisper in Josh's ear. "Watch your back mate. Watch your back."

Josh watched him leave as he necked the rest of his drink. Despite his bravado his hands were shaking.

CHAPTER 27

During the following weeks Kirsty, Lucy and Rick continued to spend time together. They were developing a strong bond but were always careful to avoid meeting at Rick's or discussing Josh. Karen remained at her mother's and despite a dreadful longing, Jack still refused to see her. Fortunately, Kirsty kept him up to date on Karen's health and well-being. He refused to allow them to pass on any information about how he was coping but she discretely managed to make her mother aware that he was struggling without her. Kirsty hoped that eventually they would find a way forward and reconcile. Lucy, on the other hand, felt her mother's actions were unforgivable.

Karen struggled with depression, stubbornly refusing to acknowledge her son in the hope that Jack would see this as a sign of her remorse.

Without any discussion Josh moved in with Mimi and they started a relationship of sorts. She loved him but he still harbored feelings for Lucy. Trying desperately to push her from his mind he threw himself wholeheartedly into his affair with Mimi.

* * *

His lips found her neck and traced the line of her throat. She moaned appreciatively as she rolled over and opened her eyes. "Hi babe," she purred.

"Shush...Roll over."

"What?"

"You heard."

"Josh, what are you doing?"

"Well duh? What do you think I'm doing?"

He slid his hand under the quilt and ran a finger up her thigh. She giggled. "That tickles."

"I know," he growled.

Pushing the covers back he took a nipple into his mouth and nibbled as he felt it harden. Her hands grabbed his buttocks and drove his hard-on against her. Even through his jeans and the duvet she could feel him. He withdrew and stood over her. She smiled as he ripped off the quilt exposing her naked body. "Jeez it's been a long six weeks. I am so ready for this," she whispered.

"You're sure?"

"God yeh. Doc says I'm ok so let's go baby." He grinned as he slowly began to undo his jeans. Taking over from him she released his throbbing cock and took the head in her mouth. He closed his eyes and shuddered. "Fucking hell, that's so good."

She withdrew her mouth but continued to work the shaft slowly. Glancing up at him from under her eye-lashes she smiled "I know."

His fingers traced a line from her naval to her freshly waxed pussy and she spread her thighs in response. Continuing to run her tongue up and down his cock she gently massaged his balls as he moaned softly. "Oh my God, that feels amazing." Putting a hand over hers he pulled away from her mouth. He looked down at his hand as he stroked her outer lips, just glimpsing the glistening purplish folds inside. "Your turn I think," he whispered as he leant down towards her and ran his tongue the length of her minge. She shuddered. She was already wet and as he took her clitoris into his mouth and sucked hungrily she grabbed his head and thrust herself onto his mouth. "Finger me," she panted. "Please."

Happy to oblige he slid a finger into the hot depths and felt her body respond as she clenched around it. As a second joined it he felt her take his throbbing penis deep into her mouth and the sensation of the warm, wetness of her, both on his face and his dick drove him to oblivion as he fought not to come in her mouth.

Reaching for a condom she rolled it over him as he fought to keep control of his pulsating cock. Without hesitation he pulled her towards him and as she mounted him he slid a hand down her body and worked her clitoris as she thrust her way to orgasm.

She collapsed on top of him and kissed him ferociously, their faces and bodies glistening with sweat. "Jesus babe, that was fantastic. Thanks." She grinned up at him. "It's nice to know everything still works so to speak."

He laughed as he kissed her nose. "All in working order as far as I'm concerned. No complaints from me."

"Thanks for everything. I really appreciate you moving in and looking after me."

"No probs. I wanted to. Even you need taking care of now and again."

"Well, it's job done for you then hun. I'm back to work tonight."

Instantly Josh pushed her away from him and sat up, holding her at arm's length, frowning. "What the fuck?"

"Hey what's the problem? It's my job ok?" She replied nonchalantly as she rolled away from him.

"No it's not fucking ok actually. There's no way you're going back there."

Anger flared in her eyes as she stood up, her hands on her hips. "Er, excuse me. Who the fuck are you to tell me what to do?"

"I'm your friend, no. It's more than that. I thought we were together, that we had something special?" She looked away as he continued. "I'm the guy who found you bleeding in the back of my limo and called the ambulance. I'm the guy who heard you crying in the night and held you till you stopped. Your days as a hooker, dancer...Whatever, are over. End of." She sat back down on the bed and took his hands in hers. "Josh I appreciate everything you've done for me and what we have is really special but I have to work and this is all I know how to do."

"Bullshit." She shrugged as he argued his case. "Try waitressing or bar work, dancing even. How about some topless work, just none of the sex and stag-party shit. Please."

"I can earn as much in a week as a topless waitress earns in a month. Why should I stop? I was unlucky. I'll just make sure I never work solo again. I've been hurt before. It wasn't the first time. I'm fine now. Honest. How about if I just work in the club where it's safe and knock the other stuff on the head? Will you be happy then? "

"No," he mumbled, "But it's a start I guess."

She stood up and angrily threw on her robe before heading downstairs. "MIMI...MIMI," he called after her as he struggled into his jeans.

As he entered the kitchen she was knocking back what looked like a large vodka. "Right...Vodka, yeh that'll help," he muttered.

"Fuck off! You're not my father so mind your own fucking business will you?" She snarled.

"No I'm not your father but I do care and there's no way you're going back out there." He whispered. She turned to face him, scarlet with anger.

"It's nothing to do with you ok? You get it. Nothing. Thanks for what you've done but I don't need you or your shit advice thank you. Feel free to move out anytime ok?"

"Fine, your choice. Just one thing?" She raised her eye brows questioningly. "The miscarriage. You said it was mine. Was that the truth or were you just saying that?"

She turned away and hung her head. Almost imperceptibly she whispered "It was the truth."

* * *

As the taxi approached the club she felt her heart begin to race and her hands start to shake. "Stupid cow," she berated herself under her breath but despite her outward confidence she knew she was scared, plain and simple.

Having changed into her working clothes she made her way to the bar. For the first time in her life she felt vulnerable and self-conscious and wished she had on a less revealing costume, despite the fact that she was wearing more than any of the other girls.

Sitting at the bar she turned her back to the room as she downed another large vodka. The ice-cubes rattling as her hand shook.

As the alcohol hit her system she felt herself calming down. "I can do this, I can do this," she muttered under her breath. After several minutes one of her regular clients took the stool, next to her and signaled for more drinks. Reaching over to kiss her cheek he smiled. "Hi, Mimi, nice to see you back. Would you like to join me for a while?" Forcing a smile she spun round and faced him. "That would be lovely, Rob." Grinning he took her hand and led her to the door leading to the private rooms.

The room was dark and smelt of sex, alcohol and stale cigarette smoke. Turning to her he slipped off his jacket and placed four £50 notes on the side table. "You dirty, filthy whore, get over here and kneel down. You disgust me." Obediently she did as he asked and as he slowly undid his flies with one hand he grabbed her hair and pulled her head back with the other. "You dirty cow," he growled. "Get your fucking lips round my cock bitch and I don't wanna feel your teeth. Understand?"

Taking him in her mouth she heard him groan and as she moved her head backwards and forwards along the shaft and ran her tongue over the throbbing end she watched his eyes close as he started to pant. Within seconds she was in the back of the limo and it wasn't the regular punter she knew and trusted who was thrusting into her mouth it was the stag and his mates and she felt herself gag. Smothering a scream she pulled away and fell backwards onto the floor, crying. Startled his eyes flew open. "What's wrong? You ok? Did I hurt you?" His face full of concern. "No...I'm fine...I'm sorry. It was just a cough and I didn't want to bite you. My fault." She attempted a smile to reassure him as she crawled over to him and took him into her mouth again. "No. I wanna fuck you. Now. Lay down and open your legs."

"Of course Sir, anything you like." Lying down on the couch she spread her legs exposing her neatly waxed pussy.

"You dirty whore look at you," he teased grinning, "not even wearing any underwear. I bet you like to touch yourself."

"Not as much as I like you touching me Sir." She purred.

"Are you wet?"

"Of course. I'm a dirty whore. I'm always wet. Feel me."

Approaching her with his penis hard and glistening in one hand he ran a finger a length of her glistening lips. "Dirty, filthy girl."

"I am."

"You need to be punished."

"Yes Sir, I do." He sniffed his finger.

"I can smell the other men on you. You've got a dirty, stinky cunt. You know that?"

His voice deepened as his hand worked his cock. "I am a *really* bad girl. I need to be taken in hand and punished," she pleaded as her hand caressed her smooth lips and grazed over her clit. "Please help, Sir. Teach me a lesson."

"I don't have a choice do I? You need to be punished. You know what to do."

Rolling over she spread her thighs and exposed her bare buttocks and glistening pussy. As the first hard slap landed she barely flinched. She heard his satisfied grunt as he raised his hand for the next one. The red hand-prints rose on her buttocks and thighs. "Ooh thank you Sir, ooh thank you Sir." She repeated as the slaps landed on her tingling flesh.

She heard the packet rip and within seconds his dick was pushing against her opening. Thrusting hard into her. Relief washed over her. It was nearly over. He would come soon, and afterwards the middle-aged bank manager would smile, apologize, buy her another drink and head back to his wife in suburbia until next time. She made the appropriate groaning noises as he pumped his way to oblivion and it was almost over when his hand slipped round the front of her face and clamped over her mouth. Leaning down he breathed into her ear, "Shut the fuck up cunt. You're not supposed to enjoy this," and instantly she was back in the limo and something inside her snapped.

She bucked and threw him off and as he landed on the floor she planted a kick straight into his bollocks. The air gushed out of him as he fell sideways clutching his traumatized genitals. Without warning she punched him in the face and blood spewed from his nose. "YOU FUCKING BASTARD!!" She screamed. "GET THE FUCK AWAY FROM ME!!" The door flew open and two doormen stood aghast as they took in the injured punter and the furious prostitute. "Mimi...Babe?" One ventured, hands extended. "You ok? What's happened? Did he hurt you?"

The other doorman was helping the punter to his feet and was trying to gather the man's clothes. "I never hurt her," the man protested as blood dripped from his face. "Honestly, I never hurt her. We were just playing. Same as usual. She just went mad. I didn't do anything wrong. I swear."

"Is that right, Mimi?"

She nodded, silently, her whole body shaking.

* * *

Amber thrust another drink into her friend's shaking hands as black mascara cascaded down her cheeks. "It's ok hun, just take deep breaths. You'll be fine."

"It doesn't feel like it. How can I work after what just happened. That poor guy. Did you see him? Amber...I don't know if I can do this anymore."

Amber crouched down in front of Mimi and took her face in her hands. "So...Go do something else."

"Like what?"

"Anything. Just not this. Maybe this was meant to be. Maybe it's time to move on. Well, at the very least move up, 'cause let's face it babe, the only way from this is up." The friends grinned at each other. "What do I tell Max?"

"Tell him you quit. Simple as."

"Do I have to give notice or something?" Amber burst out laughing.

"Oh for fuck's sake girl what are you like? This isn't bloody Tesco's you know. Of course you don't have to give notice. Just tell him you can't do this anymore after what happened. He'll understand."

"Maybe I could waitress or work behind the bar what do you think?"

"The punters know you babe, how long before you get asked to take someone out back? It's gonna be hard to refuse and what happens if they kick off? Can you deal with that? I'm not sure Max would be too happy about word getting out about tonight either. Better if you just go."

"I guess."

"That's your answer then."

"I can't just walk out. Can I?"

"You going back in there to work the club?"

"No."

"Then text Josh or call a cab. I'll tell Max."

Mimi's head flew up. "Really?"

"Sure. He'll be fine with it. Well not fine obviously 'cause the punters love you but he'll understand."

Mimi took Amber in her arms and as they clung to each other crying Mimi knew Josh had been right all along.

Eventually she dried her eyes and changed out of the PVC outfit and into her 'home clothes' and as the cab pulled away from the club she wiped the red lipstick from her mouth and threw the tissue out of the window. "Happy retirement, Mimi," she whispered.

* * *

Rick heard his son's key in the lock just as he put the phone down. "Dad? You home?"

"Hi mate. Yeh, in the kitchen. Want a brew?"

"Cheers." Rick looked over his shoulder at his son and noticed the rucksack and kitbag on the lounge floor. "Er... You moving back?"

"Yeh. That ok?"

"Sure."

"She's gone back to work at the club." Rick spun round and stared open mouthed at his son.

"What the fuck?"

"Exactly. I begged her to try something else, anything but she insisted. Dad I just couldn't handle it. We argued and she told me she was fine and that I could move out anytime so here I am." Placing a hand on Josh's shoulder Rick shook his head. "You know she didn't mean it don't you?"

"Then why say it?"

"She's probably about the most screwed up person I've ever met. She's been abused by her step-father, taken drugs, attempted suicide, been a prostitute and now been so brutally assaulted she suffered a miscarriage. She's a mess and she probably needs you more now than ever."

"Then why push me away?"

"She's scared and she probably can't cope with needing you and the fact that over the last couple of months you've seen her at her most vulnerable."

"The miscarriage..."

"Yeh?"

"She said it was mine."

"Oh shit!"

"Mmm."

"Oh son, I'm so sorry. That's awful. How do you feel about that?"

"I wished she'd have told me then maybe I could have protected her. Them. I'm not ready for a baby but she got pregnant the night I broke up with Lucy and well...I was in no mood to stop for a condom. Apparently she never goes bareback. She's known for being really careful and, allegedly, I was the one."

"That's not necessarily the case. You must know that. Anyone could have torn a condom or released semen into her prior to actual intercourse."

"I know." Josh's mobile chirped signally a text and as he read it his face paled.

"Josh?...Son?"

"Shit," he muttered.

"What's happened?"

"Sorry, Dad, that was one of Mimi's friend's from the club. Apparently she couldn't hack it and freaked out. Attacked a punter. They sent her home in a taxi. Dad, she quit."

CHAPTER 28

Struggling out of the taxi Rose was grateful to see Jack's car parked outside the house. It had been a long and expensive ride and she'd hoped he'd be home.

Ringing the doorbell she waited anxiously and when the door eventually swung open and she met his gaze she was as shocked as he was.

"Rose?"

"Jack."

"Er...You better come in." He stood aside as she made her way across the threshold. Wondering how someone could have lost so much weight in such a short time, she tried hard to hide the shock at his appearance. He shuffled into the living room and as she followed she was struck by the stale, mustiness of the room and the masses of used cups and plates that littered every surface.

"Before you start, I'm not taking her back. I don't forgive her. You're wasting your breath. Ok?"

"Fine. You do what you want. I'm quite enjoying the company actually and the extra house-keeping comes in handy so that's ok by me. No, Jack you misunderstand. I'm here to tell you the truth. Turns out I'm the only one still alive that really knows what happened and after all these years I thought you deserved to hear the real story. If you're prepared to listen that is?"

He slumped down into the armchair and hung his head in his hands. "Quite frankly, Rose I don't give a shit. My wife lied to me every day of our marriage. That's as far as I can think at the moment. I can't move past that."

"Would it help to know why?"

"I...I don't know. Yes. Maybe. No probably not. Oh fucking hell. Who cares?"

"Me. I care. My daughter's life has turned to shit. I have a grandson I don't know and by all accounts two great granddaughters I would like to meet. Karen's in pieces and by the look of you you're barely putting one foot in front of the other. Jack, it's all my fault. This whole mess is down to me and I owe it to you to tell the truth."

"You didn't make her lie."

"Yes I did. Just listen then make up your mind alright?"

"Ok. Go on then." He sighed resignedly. Rose sat opposite her son-in-law and took a deep breath.

"When she told me she was in the family-way I hit her. Did she tell you that? Anyway. I slapped her and then I hugged her. I didn't know what to do to be honest. I was so ashamed but I felt responsible too. I felt I'd let her down, not guided her in the right way to behave. I couldn't believe it had happened. My girl. Knocked-up at fifteen. I told her she had to have it adopted. No questions. Told her she would have to go to Clapham and stay with me Mum till afterwards. I just wanted her outta the way to be honest with you. I hoped she'd come back and we'd never mention it again. Anyway I thought about it and her Dad and me thought that the father shouldn't get away scott-free so the next evening I went to find him. A bloke opened the door and he looked like he'd been crying. Turns out he was the older brother and the babies' father had been killed the night before. Hit by a car in the fog. He'd been on the way to meet our Ka. They told me that the brother and his missus had been trying for a baby themselves for eight years and they offered to adopt Karen's baby there and then. I signed the paperwork and phoned 'em when the littl'un was born. They took him from the hospital and that was that. Only condition was that I had to promise that Karen would never come after the baby or try to find him. I had to promise that no-one would ever know. That the baby would be theirs and theirs alone. It wasn't hard to persuade a fifteen year old. Despite getting herself into trouble she was very childish in her ways and very shocked by the birth." Jack raised his head and stared at her.

"So basically if that bloke hadn't been killed she would have been off with him and even if the baby had been adopted she might well have tried to find him. Fucking great. So I'm the booby prize then? She obviously loved him and just settled for me. That doesn't account for the fact that she lied to *me* either. Just because she agreed to put it all behind her doesn't mean she couldn't have told me the truth."

"Well, Jack that's the hard part. I told her that if she could convince someone that she was still a virgin then she had a second chance. Someone would love her and marry her. I told her what to say, how to behave. The whole story about falling over when she was little was my idea. Once we knew you'd fallen for it I told her she'd never be able to tell you the truth. Turns out I was right," she muttered shaking her head.

"That's not fair." He barked.

"Oh so when would you have let the cat out of the bag then? On the first date, the first time you went to bed together, when you got engaged, your wedding day, first anniversary, when Kirsty was born? Go on tell me. There would never have been a right time and with every year it would have gotten harder. Don't you see? I painted her into a corner and she got stuck there. Jack, this was all my fault and I want you to forgive Karen. Please."

Angrily he stood and began pacing. "Did she put you up to this? Tell me, did she send you?"

She stood and took him by the hands. "Oh, Jack, look at you. You're in a right state. You obviously love her and she loves you. You're like a son to me and I care about both of you. Please just talk to her. You know you're breaking them girl's hearts don't you?" Pulling away he slumped back down in the chair. "Oh, Rose I really don't know what to do."

"Will you at least just ring her?"

"I don't know if I can. I feel such a pillock. She's totally humiliated me and everyone knows. I feel so ashamed." His voice cracked with emotion as he fought to hold back the tears.

"Oh, love, the only person who's ashamed is me. I made all this happen. Not our Karen. Me and her Dad, we didn't have the courage to stand by her. We were too ashamed of what people would think so we hid it all away and I lost my grand-son and she lost her baby."

"It doesn't let her off the hook for lying though, Rose. I'm her husband and yet she hid this from me." He lifted his head defiantly and looked her squarely in the eye. "She was the first girl I ever went with you know. I saved myself and I thought she'd done the same. Turns out she'd already been around the track a few times by then."

"JACK!! That's not true. She fell in love and he seduced her. She wasn't the first and she won't be the last. You of all people should know that. It happens but she wasn't a slut. She was a good girl. It was only that one bloke and she loved him."

"So she says."

"It's the truth."

"Yeh and she's so reliable ent she?"

"Jack...When you heard that your Lucy was expecting how did you feel?"

"What's that got to do with anything?"

"How did you feel? Happy, sad, angry? Weren't you even a little relieved when she lost it and you had the chance to make it all disappear?"

"Don't you fucking dare! That was my grand-child."

"Yes I know but you hated the idea of a man of his age sleeping with her and as soon as you got the chance you made sure she fell out of love with him didn't you? Don't bother to deny it 'cause Karen told me what the pair of you did. Now tell me, what's the difference? You did what you could to make it all go away, to make out like it had never happened and so did I."

Rose sighed heavily, picked up her handbag and headed for the door. Jack sat gazing out of the window refusing to meet her gaze. "Promise me you'll think about it. We're not so different you and me. We both did what we felt was right. Well, I tried. That's all I can do. You'll have to make your own mind up. I can't do no more. Would you mind ordering me a taxi please love?"

Turning to face her he frowned. "A taxi? All the way to Tower Hamlets? That'll cost you a bloody fortune."

"That's alright thank you. I can manage."

"I'm sure, but you don't have to. I'll drive you."

She smiled at him. "That would be nice. Thanks. Are you sure?" He walked over to her and hugged her warmly. "No. But I'll drive you anyway. Come on."

* * *

Amber struggled into the lounge weighed down with carrier bags. "Blimey, I had no idea I'd left so much stuff behind," Mimi responded as she took the bags from her friend.

"If I'd have realized I'd have enlisted some help I'm telling you." Both women laughed as they fell into each other's arms.

Amber held her friend at arm's length and studied her face. "So, how's things?"

"Oh you know me, I'm fine. How's you?"

"Don't worry about me mate, I'm good ta. Mmm you sure you're ok? How's thing's with Josh?"

"Great actually. He's moved back in after my tantrum and he's paying all the bills bless him. Told me to hang on to my savings."

"That's so good of him."

"I know."

"So what's the problem then? I thought you'd be happy. Oh and by the way, mine's white with two in case you've forgotten."

Mimi grinned, "That's a weird way to take wine."

"Oh, now you're talking. Yes please, babe."

As Mimi poured out two glasses of chilled white wine the women made themselves comfortable on the two leather sofas and as Mimi took her first sip Amber pulled a CD from her handbag.

"Remember this?" Mimi burst out laughing spraying wine all over her friend. "Oh my God you've still got it. Here let's have it." Taking the disc she inserted it into the player as both women sat forward in anticipation.

After several seconds a beautifully soulful female voice rang out and Amber closed her eyes and smiled. "Hun you have an amazing voice."

"Piss off."

"Seriously, you can really sing. Do you ever wish you'd stuck to that instead of...Well...What I do? What you used to do?"

"Truthfully, sometimes, but there's a sort of poetic justice in getting men to pay for the one thing my step-father took from me. Bastard. It's like I'm getting my own back on him if you see what I mean?"

"Yeh, I do. Are you gonna think about singing again now?"

"I don't know mate to be honest. I haven't really gotten past the whole drama of last week. I can't believe I went for that poor bloke. Is he ok?"

"I sat him down and told him about the attack and the miscarriage..."

"YOU DID WHAT?" Mimi's face was scarlet as she slammed her glass down. Raising her hand to appease her friend Amber continued.

"Hang on, hang on, chill. He's a decent bloke and he totally understood. Max sorted him out with free life membership and 10% discount at the bar. I thought if he understood he might not press charges. I was right."

Hanging her head in her hands, all sign of anger gone she looked so lost and afraid again. "Oh shit," she muttered. Sitting beside her Amber put her arm around her friend as fresh tears fell.

CHAPTER 29

The traffic was awful but to his credit Jack didn't complain and as they approached the tower block Rose started to feel nervous. He'd been very quiet and she hoped he was considering her words rather than just feeling tired or angry.

Pulling up outside the block he opened the door for her and as she twisted to get out of the car she caught her foot on her handbag strap and fell face-first out of the door onto the tarmac. "Oh shit, Rose...ROSE you ok?"

"Mmm I think so. Am I bleeding?" As he helped her up he saw that she'd split her lip and grazed her cheek and her knee. "Oh gawd look at you. Here, I've got a tissue." He handed her a tissue and as she dabbed at her face and studied the blood she grabbed his arm "Oh, Jack, I'm bleeding. I feel all faint. Don't let me go, don't let me go."

"Alright, alright I won't," he muttered rolling his eyes. "You're fine. It's only a scratch. Come on, let's get you upstairs."

* * *

As Rick and Sally headed for the staff car park he took her hand and kissed her knuckles. She smiled. "What was that for? Someone might see," she teased.

"Yeh and?"

"Well I thought we were supposed to be discreet?"

"We were but maybe we don't have to be now."

"Really?"

"What difference does it make after all? Married couples work together all over the hospital."

"Yeh but they're married. We're just dating. Not even living together."

"Mmm well, I think we ought to change that too."

"Huh?" He turned to face her and taking her face in his hands he kissed her deeply.

"Sal, come live with me. Let's do this properly. I love you and I wanna be with you. Simple."

Returning the kiss and feeling their passion ignite she smiled up at him. "You're sure?"

"Never been surer."

"If you have any doubts..." But her sentence was cut short by a second more passionate kiss. "Oh, Murphy, what have you done? Better get me home and seal the deal." She giggled as she pinched his buttock.

* * *

Her lip was throbbing but the bleeding had largely stopped. It felt swollen and hot and it hurt when she spoke. Likewise her knee was stinging and every step caused her pain. It occurred to her that at 80 she was perhaps a little too old for stunt work. The thought made her smile which in turn caused her lip to start bleeding again.

"Oh, Rose what we gonna do with you?" He asked as he placed her key in the lock and threw open the door for her.

He had helped the older woman to the sofa and was removing his jacket when he turned towards the kitchen door and saw her. Her face was ashen and her eyes were filled with tears. Speechless he turned away as his mother-in-law struggled to her feet. "Right you two, I'm gonna go and sort meself out and I suggest you do the same. I had to throw meself on the floor to get you both here so don't let me down." And with that she ambled into the hall, locked the front-door, and taking the key with her made her way to her bedroom. "Mum, please, this is ridiculous; you can't lock us in here like kids. Mum...MUM!!! Oh for Christ's sake. Stupid old woman."

He walked to the balcony door and stared out at the darkening city. Hearing the kettle start to boil he was reminded of all the nights before they were married they'd stood out on the balcony watching the lights, holding hands and he choked back a sob.

"Jack?" He jumped. She was right behind him. He knew that if he turned he'd be unable to hold back the tears so he stayed looking out at the night. "Jack?"

"What?"

"Look at me. Please."

"I can't."

"Please." She took hold of his shoulders and despite his resistance she slowly turned him to face her. Tears streamed down both their faces. Slowly he raised his eyes to meet hers. "Your Mum said something today that made me think. She said that what she'd done was just like what we did for Lucy when we asked Tom to treat her badly so she'd chuck him."

"Jack I'm scared to say anything in case you walk out of here and I never get to see you again. Tell me what you want me to say. I love you and I can't bear to be without you."

"I'm so angry and disappointed that you lied but I think I understand now. Your Mum didn't give you a choice did she? When would you have been able to tell me? There would never have been a right time. There's one thing I have to know and I want the truth whether it's gonna hurt or not. You have to promise you won't lie just to please me ok?"

"Ok," she replied sobbing.

"If he hadn't been killed would you have tried to find him? Even after you and me got together? Even after the girls were born?"

Karen took a deep breath and took her husband's hands in hers. "I swear, when I told you I loved you I meant it. I never lied about how I felt about you and 'cause I loved you...Love you, I never wanted to find him. Yes I was heartbroken that he never turned up that day. Of course I was, but I was with him because I was pregnant and I was with you because I love you. With him it was a knee-jerk reaction. Oh shit I'm pregnant. With you it was my choice. Always was, always will be."

He nodded once and let her hands drop as he turned away. "Jack...JACK? Talk to me, please."

"Ka I always loved you. That was never in question was it? It was about you choosing me. Now I think I understand why you did what you did. I believe you love me."

"So why are you walking away from me?"

He turned and walked back towards her and taking her face in his hands he kissed her softly, both of them tasting their tears. "We need to pack your stuff and get you home but first we ought to see to your Mum. She gave herself a right ole clonk. Bless her." She laughed as she held him tightly. "She's too bloody clever for her own good if you ask me."

* * *

Opening the front-door he stopped and listened. Above the sound of Mimi and Amber giggling and chatting he could hear music. A woman singing but he didn't recognize the voice. It seemed to be an album of covers and as he took off his coat and shoes he found himself humming.

"Ladies,"

"Hi, Josh."

"Hi hun, good day?"

He leant in to kiss Mimi and Amber grinned as she picked up on the sexual chemistry in the room.

"Yeh it was ok ta. What you listening to?"

Mimi shot forward from the sofa and pressed the stop button on the CD player.

"What the fuck?"

Amber frowned at her friend. "What did you switch it off for? Let him listen. It's good."

"Shut up."

"Er girls would someone like to tell me what just happened?"

Amber sighed and restarted the CD. "It's Mimi, she made a demo disc years ago. Before we started working at the club. She was looking for work as a singer but there wasn't anything going. She's good though eh?"

Aghast he turned to face her and getting down on his knees he took her hands in his and kissed them. "You're amazing. Why didn't you tell me you could really sing? You daft mare." Pulling her hands away she stood and walked into the kitchen. Both he and Amber shrugged and he got up and followed her. "Babe?"

"Piss off."

"Nice...Classy." She burst out laughing.

"You bugger. Why do you always do that?"

"What?"

"Make me laugh when I'm pissed off with you?"

"Well duh? Don't really want you to be pissed off at me. Tried it once. Didn't really like it."

She laughed as he slipped his arms around her waist. "Seriously though, I can't believe I've never heard you sing. Not even in the shower."

She grinned up at him, "Well to be honest we're usually busy doing other things in the shower and it's hard to sing with your mouth full."

* * *

Rick's lips grazed her shoulder as he slid her bra-strap down. As he exposed her breast he leant down and licked her nipple then softly blew on it. She giggled as he watched it harden. Repeating the process with the other nipple he gazed longingly at her breasts and taking them in his hands he rubbed his thumbs over the pert, pink nipples as a moan escaped her lips. "Take it off," he breathed and silently the garment slipped to the floor. "And the rest." Again she obeyed, wordlessly as she used her fingers to slowly slide the thong down to her ankles. He looked her up and down. "Mmm, gorgeous." They smiled at each other as she began by taking her breasts in her hands and caressing her nipples as she closed her eyes. One hand slid cautiously down her body to the neatly sculpted tuft and as she casually spread her thighs she began to ease her fingers between her moist lips. Throwing her head back she moaned again as her fingertips grazed her clitoris. "Are you wet?"

"Yes," she purred.

"Lay down." Opening her eyes she walked backwards towards the bed and, without breaking eye-contact spread herself on the quilt.

"I'm gonna lick you till you scream." She grinned up at him as she reached for his zip. Releasing his throbbing cock she leant forward and licked the glistening dew-drop from the end. "Promises, promises," she teased.

Within seconds he had shed his clothes and was sliding onto the bed next to her and as he slid a hand along her thigh she rolled on to her back and spread her legs for him. He growled his appreciation as his hand drifted towards her glistening pink folds. Running his fore-finger along her sensitive inner lips he casually caressed her clitoris. Instantly she pushed her hips against his finger. Grinning he let the finger fall until it traced the outline of her sopping wet opening. He felt the heat as he let his finger slide inside her. Again she rocked against him and as he let a second finger join the first he felt her body pulsate as her climax approached. Aware of how close she was he leant down and as he slid his fingers into her he lapped at her clitoris until she came.

As her orgasm abated he raised his face to smile at her. She was flushed and her hair was stuck to her damp forehead. She still clutched the sheet in both fists.

Feeling his climax approaching fast he stroked her cheeks with his thumbs. "I wanna be inside you," he growled. She nodded once and turned round until her buttocks faced him. Almost unable to hold on he took a minute to close his eyes and focus. The glistening pink folds peeking out from between her arse cheeks were irresistible and as he traced the line of her pussy with his thumb and felt the warm wetness he struggled not to come.

Parting her lips he inched himself into her and as she opened to him he felt her shudder beneath him. Reaching forward to hold her breasts as they moved their bodies together he felt a huge wave of love and passion engulf him as he felt her come again. Suddenly the realization that he was losing his hard-on washed over him. He felt for her nipples and screwed his eyes up as he pictured her glistening, pink pussy. It didn't help. He felt himself softening inside her.

Eventually they collapsed together and kissed deeply. It was then that she noticed he had tears in his eyes. Lifting up on one arm she reached forward to wipe his face. "Babe, what's wrong? Are you ok?"

"Oh Sweetheart," he smiled into her concerned face, "I was just a little overcome with emotion thinking about how much I love you. That's all." Immediately Sally threw her arms around his neck and smothered his face in kisses as she began to cry.

* * *

The limo pulled slowly through the West End traffic. The city lights banished all semblance of night and the streets were alive with people. His heart was thumping as he pulled up outside the hotel and opened the door for his client.

As he indicated to pull out he switched on the CD player and Mimi's voice filled the car. After several minutes the intercom buzzed. "Yes Sir?" Josh responded.

"What CD is this you're playing?"

"Er...It's a new artist Sir. She's as yet, unsigned." Josh waited for the inevitable fall-out. He knew he'd taken a massive risk and could possibly lose his job. Although he didn't believe it was possible he was sure his heart rate had increased as the sweat trickled down the back of his neck.

"Driver...Let me get this right; you have used your position to force me to listen to your girl-friend's caterwauling. I take it you don't really like your job?" Switching the music off Josh cursed his stupidity under his breath. "I'm so sorry Sir. Forgive me. I was listening to it on the way to pick you up and I didn't realize the disc was still in the player. My apologies."

"Oh for God's sake do you really expect me to believe that?"

"Sir...I...Er..."

"Oh shut up and switch the CD back on. Might as well have a proper listen to it I suppose."

"Yes Sir," Josh gasped as he found the switch.

Long minutes passed as Mimi's voice filled the limo. The passenger was silent. Eventually Josh pulled the car into the space outside the award ceremony and as he opened the door the record producer passenger held out his hand, palm upwards. Josh started at it, confused. "Sir?"

"The disc idiot, give me the fucking disc. I presume you can give me her contact details?"

Grinning Josh slid his palm into his jacket pocket and withdrew a disc with all Mimi's phone numbers on the cover and handed it to the producer grinning. "Mmm very smooth. But if you ever pull a stunt like this again I'll have you fired. Understand?"

"Yes Sir."

"FYI...You've quite possibly changed your girl-friend's life forever," and before Josh could reply, the producer had disappeared.

Part 3

CHAPTER 30

Rick and Sally pulled up outside the tower block and gazed up towards the 20th floor. "Shit, I hope the bloody lift's working." Sally muttered.

"I just hope it doesn't smell of piss." Rick replied as he nudged her elbow. They both smiled nervously. Turning towards him she took his face in her hands and gazed into his eyes. "You sure you're ok with this?" Silently he nodded. "Right then, let's go."

The ride up in the lift seemed to take forever as they huddled in the center of the graffittied, stained, malodourous metal box as it clunked and juddered upwards. Eventually they arrived and as they walked out onto the balcony both of them stopped to fill their lungs with fresh air. Rick bent to kiss Sally softly and she took his hand.

As they approached the door Rick slowed, hesitating on the walkway. He took a deep breath and turned to look out over the city. "Babe?" she whispered.

"I'm ok, just need a minute that's all. Last time I saw *her* was the day I hit my head and it wasn't a great meeting. Guess I'm just a little suspicious of the change of heart. Meeting her Mum too? My *Nan*, the one who arranged the adoption, the one who told Karen she couldn't keep me. The one who made her lie to Jack. What kind of a woman gives a fifteen year old that kind of ultimatum?"

"One who thought she was doing her best but got it wrong," came the voice from behind them. They both spun round. "Hello, I'm Rose, I'm your Nan." The door had opened whilst they'd been talking and Rose stood in the doorway. Both Rick and Sally blushed. Sally stepped forward first and held out her hand. "Hi, Rose, sorry about that. I'm Sally." The old woman shook her hand and gave her a quick glance but her main interest was obviously Rick. Her eyes were misted as he reached out to shake her hand.

Gripping his hand between hers he saw her visibly sag as she leant into the door-jamb. "Rose, it's good to finally meet you. I'm sorry you heard all that. I didn't mean to upset you." Maintaining her hold she smiled "It's fine, it don't really matter. You're quite right really. Me and her Dad, we did get it wrong. Can't change it now. I'm just trying to make it right."

"I know," he whispered softly, "and I appreciate it. I really do."

"Come on in, straight down to the end. Make yourselves at home." she said stepping aside.

As they entered the small but very tidy living room both Jack and Karen stood up. Jack stepped forward immediately and greeted them both warmly whilst Karen hung back sheepishly. Rick turned his gaze to his mother and as their eyes met both immediately misted with tears. Sally, Rose and Jack slipped silently from the room into the adjacent kitchen.

* * *

The tube train rattled noisily through the tunnels as Josh's I-pod played Mimi's debut album through the ear-phones. He smiled. She was a big star now. Living in the states, a new name, a new identity. Mimi the whore was dead and Casey Wright was alive and well and topping the charts. Her new record producer knew about her past as did the record company but they'd staged such a successful cover up even Mimi's friends had a job recognizing her. Closing his eyes he let his mind drift back to the last time she'd stopped over in London. She'd text him her hotel room number and when he'd arrived she'd been waiting for him dressed in a tiny lace slip. She'd slowly undressed him and as she'd slid his jeans off she's slipped his throbbing cock into her mouth and toyed with the end with her tongue as she gazed up at him provocatively, caressing his balls. Unable to wait he'd lifted her up and carried her to the bed as she nibbled his neck.

Laying her full length he'd slid the silky slip from her body and had gazed at her, admiring both the familiar tattoos, and the new as well as the piercings he remembered so well. Her nipples already hard, had tasted sweet and she had arched her back to meet his mouth. He'd clasped her hands above her head as he'd run his tongue the length of her body to tease her sculpted tuft, easing her thighs apart.

Her silky thighs had spread easily as he'd buried his face into her soft, moist, glistening folds. The taste and smell of her driving his cock almost to the point of no return. She'd shuddered beneath him as his tongue had grazed her clitoris. He'd eased one finger into her as she responded he eased a second and a third. She was tight and hot and he worked her pussy until he felt her squeeze on his fingers as her orgasm approached.

The carriage clattered as he smiled to himself, instantly recalling the taste and feel of her. He rearranged his work bag on his lap to hide his hard-on.

Nudging her lips with his cock he'd felt her open up to him. Looking into each other's eyes they'd smiled knowingly as he'd thrust into her, inch by inch, so very slowly. She'd been unbelievably hot and wet and he'd felt his climax building. Reaching down to her clitoris she began to stroke herself and as she'd felt herself come she'd closed her eyes and thrust against him as her thighs wrapped around him.

He opened his eyes to check the station and happy that he had time he closed his eyes, listened to her voice and returned to the memory.

She'd kissed him and he'd noticed tears. He'd asked her what was wrong, he'd known better than to ask if he'd hurt her. He'd hurt her a bit and she'd liked it. That was *her* thing. That was understood. She's shaken her head and slowly explained that she'd started seeing someone else. Someone she really liked. Someone who didn't know her as a whore, someone who didn't hurt her 'cause now, that wasn't really *her* thing anymore. He'd nodded and kissed her. Happy and sad in equal measure.

It was over and they both knew it.

* * *

"How are you? After your op I mean?"

"Erm...Ok I suppose. You? How's your head?"

"Yeh, fine thanks. Mind if I sit down?" She smiled and gestured towards the sofa.

"Course not, sorry."

"Thanks." Her hands were shaking and her eyes seemed to be tracing every corner of the room in order to avoid meeting his gaze. "Karen...Karen?" Her eyes stopped wandering and settled on his. "Karen, we need to talk. I gather you've sorted everything out with Jack?"

"Yes, I've got my Mum to thank for that, bless her, she spoke to him and made him see things differently, then she got him here. Do you know she threw herself out of the car face first in order to get him to help her up here to the flat just so we could talk. She locked us in the flat until we'd sorted ourselves out. She's a hard nut but she's got a big heart." Rick laughed.

"I'd like to get to know her and I know my kids would too."

"She's hoping to spend some time with you too."

"Jack told me all about what happened, with Rose, how she gave you no choice. Why you gave me up and why you wanted to protect your secret. I get it now. I understand." A sob escaped her as she hung her head and covered her face with her hands. Hurrying to her side he placed an arm around her as she leant into him and wept. "Oh, Karen, I'm sorry. I didn't mean to upset you."

Eventually the sobbing subsided and she turned to face him. "You're so like him; your father. I'm so sorry for what I said to you at the hospital. I still stupidly thought I could keep all this under wraps. None of this is your fault. I always knew that but I felt so exposed and out of control, like my world was going to come crashing down. Unfortunately, it did," she smiled ruefully.

"How's things with Lucy?" She sighed and shook her head, more tears threatening.

"Terrible. She still misses Josh and she sees this as all my fault. She say that if I'd been honest in the beginning they'd never have dated and she wouldn't have fallen for him. I've found my son and lost my daughter. What a bloody mess." Rick took her hand and nodded. He remembered Josh and Lucy's reaction to the news. "That's something we can't change. Nothing can."

"That's the worst thing. Mum's spoken to her but she just won't forgive me. She's still stopping at Kirsty's."

"I know. I see them quite often and they go out with my daughters too. It's great to see them all together. The twins are adorable. You must be so proud."

"I am, they're gorgeous. Did you know Kirsty had to have a termination a while back? It was some kind of severe birth defect. It broke everyone's heart, especially hers. It was such a bad time for us. Then Lucy met up with Tom and got pregnant and had a miscarriage. He was a lot older than her and it was a disaster really. That broke her heart. She took a long time to recover and then to find out the next person you fall for is your nephew. Well no wonder she hates me."

"She doesn't hate you; she just needs time, that's all."

The door opened tentatively and Sally's face appeared. "Tea?" They both smiled and replied simultaneously. "Please."

CHAPTER 31

Josh hurried in through the staff entrance of the club and changed into his black suit, white shirt and black tie. Having attached his radio to his lapel he headed for the front door of the club.

"Hi mate, long time no see. How's things?"

"Yeh good ta," he replied. "Anything major due tonight?"

His colleague shook his head, "Don't think so, couple a stag parties but nothing too heavy. Did you hear about that bloke who used to work here?... Shit what's his name? The head doorman. He moved up to Manchester to work."

"You don't mean Eddie?"

"Yeh, that's him, seems he got into a bit of trouble last week. Some blokes from down this way were up in Manchester for the weekend and they kicked the shit outta him, fractured skull, possible brain damage, broke both his hands. Real nasty." Josh felt his blood run cold as sweat began to prickle his skin. "Eddie, the Eddie who used to work here?"

"Yes. That's what I said."

"Did they get the blokes that did it?"

"No. No-one saw or heard anything by all accounts."

"Holy fuck. Is he gonna be ok?"

"Don't know yet. He's in intensive care."

Josh's head started to pound as he checked various club members ID's without really seeing them. The evening passed in a blur. Josh spoke to people and greeted guests and club members but could recall none of them.

Eventually the evening came to an end. Josh closed the door on another departing taxi as the club members began to leave. Laughing and joking they descended the stairs behind him and crowded onto the pavement. Taxi's came and went and he helped the drunken guests into the back seats. As he slammed the rear door on the final taxi he turned and glanced up the street. Two well-dressed men were striding confidently towards him. They were chatting and laughing, seemingly oblivious to his presence. As they drew closer to the club doorway one of them stopped and turned to him. "Hi, it's Josh isn't it?" He stuck out his hand and after a moments hesitation in which he struggled to recall the man, Josh reciprocated. Both men smiled warmly. "Hi, we haven't met but I've heard a lot about you. I've been up in Manchester." The man's grip on Josh's hand tightened. Josh reached forward with his other hand and grabbed the man's wrist in an effort to free himself. As the second man grabbed and secured Josh's left hand he felt the surge of adrenaline as panic seized him. "Eddie sends his regards," he growled into Josh's ear. Instantly he felt several punches connect with his gut. Feeling the air rush out of him he collapsed against the wall as the men let him go, sprinting away laughing. Josh felt a burning sensation. It felt strange, like a punch but deeper. He felt his legs give way as he descended to his knees in slow motion. He touched his stomach and brought his palm up to his face. It was scarlet.

Then he closed his eyes.

* * *

Lucy screamed in her sleep as the knife slid into her stomach. Sitting up she flicked on the light and ran her hands over her abdomen. Nothing. The dream had been so real so vivid. She felt the pain of the knife still. Eventually she fell back asleep as silent tears soaked into her pillow.

* * *

Running into the emergency department, he burst through the double doors, breathless and wide-eyed. Gripping the counter he scanned the room for a familiar face. "My son... Josh Murphy...He's been stabbed...Where is he?" A man in scrubs approached and placing a hand on his shoulder, tried to lead him towards the relative's room. Shrugging him off Rick turned. "Malcolm, thank fuck. Where is he? I just need to see him. Just tell me what's happening."

The man shook his head sadly. "Rick, I'm sorry you're too late."

CHAPTER 32

Lucy turned the key in the lock and the familiar smells and sounds of home enveloped her.

Ever since receiving her father's invitation she'd been dreading this visit. He'd asked her if he and her mother could meet with her and talk. Everyone else was talking again and she'd felt pressurized into agreeing.

"Luce? We're in the kitchen love," he called.

Slowly, slowly she hung up her coat and turned towards the back of the house.

She heard the kettle boil as she entered and saw her mother sitting at the table. She looked drawn, anxious and tired and Lucy instantly felt guilty and for a second she imagined throwing herself into her Mum's arms and making all the pain go away, for herself and both of them. Her father looked at her, his eyes full of hope and encouragement.

"Hello love? Tea?"

"Mmm please." She pulled out the chair opposite her mother and eased herself down.

Karen started to ease a hand towards her daughter but quickly withdrew it and placed it in her lap.

Jack put three mugs on the table, sat down between the two women and, reaching for their hands, smiled reassuringly and began.

"Lucy, Mum and I are back together. Properly. We've sorted out our problems and we're trying to make it work," he turned to his wife. "Aren't we love?" She nodded, silently. "A lot of water's passed under the bridge since your Mum was fifteen and now I've spoken to your Nan I know why she did what she did. I forgive her and I don't understand why it's more of a problem for you than it is for me."

Lucy raised her head, pulled her hand away and looked her father straight in the eye. "You don't understand? YOU DON'T UNDERSTAND? THAT'S FUCKING CLEAR!"

"Lucy, please," her mother implored.

"Lucy, please," she mimicked. "What's wrong with you, Dad? She lied, not just once but for years and years, she tricked you and used you. I slept with her grandson. HER FUCKING GRANDSON. YOU'RE DAMN RIGHT YOU DON'T UNDERSTAND."

Jack took a deep breath and took hold of his daughter's hand again.

"Lucy, look at me." His voice was hard and stern and Lucy knew from the tone that her father was struggling to keep his temper in check. "The issue with Josh is not about Mum and me or about you and your Mum." She opened her mouth to speak but he raised his hand to quieten her. "Hang on, hang on, let me finish. Mum wasn't responsible for you meeting Josh and even if she'd been completely open with us you might still have fancied Josh and gotten hurt. I know you slept with him. Don't wanna be reminded of that either thanks very much but that wasn't Mum's fault. It was the fall-out, a consequence of her actions. She loves you and I want you two to talk. Not shout. Talk. I'm gonna leave you two alone and you're gonna sort it ok? That's not a question by the way. Right."

He stood and left the room.

Karen cleared her throat. "I have one question and I want you to answer it truthfully please."

"Ok."

"Did you tell Josh about getting pregnant with Tom?"

* * *

"He's in theatre, you just missed him. Sorry, Rick. Go on up to ITU and wait if you like. They're expecting you."

The breath had exploded out of Rick's lungs before he even realized he'd been holding it. Sliding down the wall he felt blackness engulf him. He heard the feet, the voices and felt the hands lifting him onto the trolley but drifted into unconsciousness anyway.

* * *

"What's that got to do with anything?"

"Did you?"

"I told him a bit about Tom, yes."

"A bit? What's that? Does he know you were carrying another man's child and if you hadn't miscarried you'd be with him now?"

"That's not fair."

"Isn't it?"

"What's the difference, Lucy? Really? If your baby had lived you'd be with Tom. You were in love with him. Anyone you have kids with in the future will have the right to know you've been pregnant by someone else before. If you chose to tell them that is."

"It's not the same. It's not. You lied..."

"Yeh and if you don't tell him or anyone else, you'd be lying too."

"Not telling isn't lying...Oh shit...It's not the same, Mum, it's not, IT'S NOT!... It's not." Huge, shuddering sobs came from Lucy as Karen made her way over to her daughter.

"This pain is about losing Josh, it's not about me or Rick or your Dad. I made a mistake love. A huge mistake and I'm paying for it and I'll be paying for it every day but this is about you and Josh. Honestly." Lucy turned her tear-stained face to her mother and knew this was the truth. Slowly she allowed her hands to creep around her mother's shoulders and as Karen embraced her she leant into the hug and wept.

The door cracked open and Jack's face appeared. He smiled at his wife.

Taking both women in a huge cuddle he kissed their foreheads tenderly. "Come home love. We miss you. Please."

CHAPTER 33

"Rick...Can you hear me?... He's opening his eyes."

"His BP's coming up and his SATS are improving. You can probably turn the oxygen down a bit now. Thanks."

Rick opened his eyes to see the A&E doctor leaning over him. He was suddenly aware of the oxygen mask on his face. "Hi, Rick, you passed out. You dropped your BP but you're ok now. Must have been the rush to get over here and the shock I guess. How you feeling?"

"Josh?"

"He's in theatre."

"You said I was too late..."

"Yes they've just taken him upstairs."

A sob escaped Rick as he took the mask from his face and tried to sit up. "You fucking arsehole, Malcolm. I thought he was dead."

"Excuse me? I never said..."

"You said I was too late...You said he'd gone...I thought he was really gone. Dead. Fucking hell, get this shit off me," he snarled as he forced his way off of the trolley.

* * *

The equipment beeped and whirred in the dimly lit ITU. Staff whispered and ventilators hissed rhythmically. Rick sat at one side of Josh's bed and Elaine sat at the other, both holding his hands. Both looked exhausted and drained. An assortment of plastic cups, soft drink bottles and sandwich wrappers lay on the bed-table. Evidence of the length of their stay. Their clothes were creased and grubby but both refused to leave. A family room had been made available but remained unused.

Two nurses approached the bed carrying a unit of blood and smiled at Rick and Elaine. "Hi, we've had the results of Josh's check Hb and it's still only 7.2 so we're gonna give him another unit ok?"

"Fine," muttered Rick, "carry on."

The nurses approached the bed-side and spoke to the un-conscious figure as if he was about to wake at any minute.

"Ok, right, Josh we're gonna give you some more blood so we're just gonna check your wrist-band ok?" The nurse picked up Josh's wrist and began reading his details. Rick stood up and began pacing around the bed-space, yawning and stretching.

"... unit number....Patients blood group B negative..." Suddenly Rick spun round and faced the bed.

"What?"

"Sorry?" Both nurses looked up.

"What did you say Josh's blood group was?"

"It's B negative," one replied.

"It can't be."

"Sorry we have the paperwork here." The nurse offered Rick the documentation. Fastidiously he poured over the drug chart, cross match slip and blood unit. Shaking his head more furiously with every second. "No, no, no...That's wrong."

His ex-wife looked up wearily. "Rick? What's the problem?" Turning to Elaine he thrust the paperwork at her.

"Here, read this. They're trying to give our son the wrong blood. They're trying to kill him. Fucking hell!" She took the paperwork and shook her head at him.

"Rick please, I don't believe that for one minute. What are you on about?" He sighed and started to explain. "I'm group O, you're group A and they're trying to give him group B blood when he can't possibly be group B. Look the paperwork is wrong." Elaine scrutinized the forms and turning to the nurses she smiled apologetically. "I'm a little tired, can you explain how this works please? Shouldn't Josh be the same as one of us?"

"Yes he should." Came a voice from behind them. As all four turned as one of the ITU consultants approached. "Er, Rick, could you keep the noise down please. What's the problem?" Taking the paperwork from Elaine he took a deep breath and started to explain. "Dr Griffin, there's been a mistake with Josh's bloods. The labs basically cocked-up and he's been allocated a unit of the wrong blood group."

The doctor held out his hand and studied the documentation. "What are you saying?"

"Josh can't be group B. I'm O and Elaine's A therefore he can't be group B. Simple. Thank God I was here. You could have killed him. After all he's been through. I just don't fucking believe it." Elaine stood up and placed a reassuring hand on his arm.

"That can't be right, Rick, Josh has already had several units in A&E and theatre and he's been fine." Rick sighed with exasperation, shook her arm from his hand, ran his hands over his face and took a deep breath. "Holy shit, Elaine, don't you know anything? As an emergency they would have given him O neg. Universal donor. Fucking wake up. Everyone knows that." He tutted loudly as he rolled his eyes. Elaine blushed and stepped back. The consultant frowned. "Look, Rick shall we go into my office and sort this out. You're disturbing the unit."

"NO FUCKING WAY. YOU THINK I'M LEAVING MY SON ALONE WHILST YOU TRY TO GIVE HIM THE WRONG BLOOD!"

"Rick, please just calm down," Elaine pleaded.

"SHUT UP, 'LAINE. YOU'VE GOT NO FUCKING IDEA WHAT'S GOING ON."

"Mr Murphy, either we take this conversation to the office or I'm getting security to escort you from the hospital. Your choice." The consultant's voice was like a knife slicing through his anger. Rick blinked several times. "I...How do I know you're not gonna just give him that blood as soon as my back's turned?... Please just get another group and save. Give him O neg in the meantime. Please. Please."

"Exactly what we're going to do, Rick. Trust me, please. We'll send this unit back to the blood bank, I'll prescribe a unit of O neg and we'll get more bloods taken. Ok?" Rick nodded solemnly as he slunk down onto the plastic chair. "Rick, we still need to talk in my office. Now." Without waiting for a reply Dr Griffin turned on his heal and walked away. Silently and wearily Rick stood and followed.

* * *

"Sit down," he said as he gestured towards the empty chair. Taking a deep breath he began softly as if struggling to keep his temper under control. "Firstly, I know how stressed and tired you are but I will not tolerate another scene like that in this unit. You're a professional, you know better than anyone that this is not the place to shout. You have a problem, you talk to someone. Did you really think we'd put that blood up once you'd identified a problem. Really?" Rick hung his head.

"No...Yes, I don't know. Christ I barely know what day it is at the moment." The consultant nodded sympathetically. "All I kept thinking was what if I hadn't been here? What if it had been Elaine or the girls on their own? My son would quite likely have died." He lifted his head up and met the doctor's gaze squarely. "You scared the shit out of me. That was such a close call." Dr Griffin stood up and walked round the desk and perched on the front.

"Definitely. But if you were me, what be going through your head about now? Honestly?"

Rick frowned. "What are you talking about?"

"Rick, try and look at this from a nursing point of view."

"What are you trying to say?" Dr Griffin sighed, stood up and made his way over to the window. Staring out at the car park for several moments he suddenly turned. "Ok. What if the group and save comes back the same?"

"It won't, but if it did, the Trust's got a fucking major problem in the labs." The doctor shook his head. "Not necessarily."

"How else can you explain your cock-up?"

"What if it's not a cock-up?"

"Well, the only way that could be true is if mine and Elaine's blood groups were wrong and as we've been donors for years we know our groups. Here, I have the card in my wallet." Rick leant forward to retrieve his wallet from his back pocket. The doctor waved the gesture away. "That won't be necessary. I believe you. You're O and Josh's mother is A. Got that. But that's not the only way is it?"

"Well, not the *only* way but...No..." Rick's face flushed as his anger rose to the surface. "HOW DARE YOU...Don't tell me you're trying to suggest he's not my son?" The doctor held up his hands in an attempt to calm Rick down.

"Think about it, Rick. I don't want to go down this road but if the bloods come back the same it's the only possibility."

"THEY WON'T."

"Ok but what if?"

* * *

Lucy sighed and pushed the quilt away. His lips brushed her neck and she felt his breath tickle her skin. She giggled. Kissing her deeply he slid a hand down to her breast and taking her nipple between his thumb and finger began to work the pert nub. She moaned in response. She was already wet and she kicked the quilt off of the bed, exposing her body to the cool air. He smiled down at her. "Hi gorgeous."

His lips grazed her throat and gently dropped the most delicate butterfly kisses the length of her body stopping only to take her nipples in his mouth and suck each one in turn. She arched her back to meet his mouth as her arousal heightened. His hands slid down the sides of her body and stopped at her hips. "Lift up for me." He whispered. She obeyed and he slipped his hands under her buttocks and lifted her pussy to meet his face. Gently he blew on her glistening, pink lips and she both shivered and giggled. He smiled up at her. "You like?"

"Mmm." He blew again and slowly ran his tongue then length of her delicate folds. She tasted so sweet. She was already dripping wet as he lapped at her, tasting her musky juice on his tongue. She moaned in response and, placing his tongue at her opening he pushed it softly inside her. She was hot and wetter than ever and he felt her moisture on his face.

Lifting her further up he placed his index fingers against her arse and began to gently tickle her. Again she shivered as another moan escaped her lips. He felt her shudder as her orgasm approached. "Finger me." She panted. "Please... Finger me."

As his finger eased into her minge he felt his balls tighten as his cock shuddered. She pushed against his hand and her pussy tightened around his finger. Sliding the second and subsequently the third deep into her he felt his climax approaching. Taking deep breaths he tried to focus on Lucy's pleasure. She was close. Her hips were rocking against his hand and she was gripping the sheet with both hands unable to speak. One flick and she'd come, just one little clit flick and he'd tip her over the edge.

Carefully he moved his body without removing his fingers and placed himself where he could slide into her. He slowly slid two fingers out and eased his cock into place. The heat and the wetness of her body stunned him still. Easing the last finger out he took over the rhythm with his cock, as he pushed himself into her depths. She opened her eyes and stared at him. "It's ok, relax," he whispered reassuringly and he felt her body relax onto him. She closed her eyes and threw back her head. He pumped her for several moments until; unable to bear it any longer he slipped his fingers between her lips and found her clitoris, hard and proud. As he stroked the tiny nub she bucked from the bed and came. Hard. Her hips pumping at him as her fanny grasped at his cock. Allowing himself to join her he pushed into her and felt his release as he came with her. She opened her eyes and looked down the bed at herself. She was naked

and uncovered, her thighs were spread and, as she exam-
ined herself she felt wet and extremely aroused. "Josh," she
murmured as she slid her fingers over her hot, wet pussy
and drifted back to sleep.

* * *

His eyes flickered rapidly as his erection pushed against
the sheet. His fists gripped the edges of the mattress and
he bucked from the bed. "JOSH!... Oh God, NURSE, HELP."
"What's the matter, Elaine?"
"It's Josh, I think he's having a seizure." Josh's nightshift
nurse; Ian studied his patient and laid a reassuring arm on
Josh's shoulder. "It's ok big guy, you're safe. Can you give
us a minute please, Elaine. I just want to re-make the bed
and do his obs. Nothing to worry about."
"Ok. He's alright isn't he? Really?" He smiled.
"He's fine; we've reduced his sedation today so he's a
bit livelier. The CT scan today was fine so I reckon he was
just dreaming or maybe his catheter is kinked. Won't take a
second to check." He smiled reassuringly at her. "Honestly."
Elaine nodded once and headed for the relatives room and
coffee machine.
"Josh, Josh, open your eyes for me mate. That's it." Josh's
eyes flickered and struggled to open. "Come on, time to
wake up." Josh persevered and eventually his eyes opened
and he stared at Ian. "Hi there, how you doing? Having a
bit of a racey dream there mate. Gave your Mum a bit of a
scare." Both men smiled and Josh whispered his first word
since the stabbing. "Lucy."

CHAPTER 34

The sound of his mobile ringing cut through his restless sleep and as soon as he saw the caller ID he sat bolt upright in bed. "Hello?"

"Rick, hi, it's Seb Griffin. I'm afraid the results have come back the same. I had the group and save repeated again just to be sure. That's three times now. I'm really sorry but I have to go with my gut and it's telling me the problem isn't in the lab."

Rick ended the call without responding.

* * *

She came awake to the sound of her doorbell ringing repeatedly and the sound of Rick shouting.

"ELAINE! ELAINE, OPEN THE FUCKING DOOR!"

"What the hell? Shit. HANG ON, RICK. I'M COMING." She stumbled to find her dressing gown and rushed down the stairs. As he saw her face through the glass panel Rick took his finger from the doorbell. Throwing open the door she squinted at the sunshine. "What's happened? Have I overslept? Has something happened? Is it Josh?" He pushed the door wide open causing it to slam against the wall, and strode past her down the hall. She blinked, shook her head and quietly shut the door before following him. "Would you mind telling me what the problem is please?"

"You fucking bitch!" He snarled, his face scarlet with barely controlled fury.

"Excuse me!"

"YOU FUCKING LYING BITCH. AFTER ALL THESE YEARS."

"Richard, what the hell are you on about? Please just tell me. You're scaring me."

"YOU KNOW EXACTLY WHAT I'M ON ABOUT. DID YOU REALLY THINK I'D NEVER FIND OUT? YOU FUCKING WHORE!"

Elaine pulled out a chair and sank down wearily. "I know you're pissed off with me but please, I haven't slept since God knows when and I'm shattered so, a little less volume and a little more info would be good. Want coffee?"

"What?... Er...Coffee? Yes please." He frowned at her. "Are you playing me or do you really not know what this is all about? Truthfully, 'Lainey please. God knows I fucking deserve it."

"Truthfully. I don't have the foggiest idea what you're on about. Let me make some coffee and then perhaps you'll tell me. OK?"

* * *

Amy and Chloe sat either side of the bed and held their brother's hands. Since waking up Josh had been moved to a side-room on the colo-rectal ward. He was weak but stable. He looked from one to the other in total amazement. "Really?" He croaked, "It's really been a week?"

"We always knew you were a lazy bastard but sleeping for a week that's good going even for you." He smiled at Amy as he squeezed her hand.

"Cheeky cow. I was bloody sedated thank you, not sleeping...How are Mum and Dad coping?"

The girl's eyes met and Chloe answered. "They've been here every night. The rest of us have been coming in the daytime when they go home to grab a couple of hours sleep and a shower. They're amazing. When you first came in they never left you. For the first two or three days they were always here."

"Jesus."

"Yeh," Amy responded. "They were really scared. We all were. You lost a shitload of blood, and you'd had such a massive op. Well, you were really rough. They thought they were gonna lose you. Didn't the doctors tell you that you lost so much blood you arrested in the ambulance? Might have known you were only after a bit of attention."

"You just bloody wait till I'm back on my feet." Leaning over to kiss his forehead his sister whispered in his ear. "I can't wait. Love you."

"Love you too, both of you." His stoma gurgled and farted and the girls laughed. Josh blushed. "Bloody thing, never says pardon either. No fricking manners. They suggested I name it, any ideas?"

"Ooh, I know, I know," squealed Amy, "name it after that bloke I went out with last year. He was full of shit. Call it Dan." All three burst out laughing and Josh reached for a pillow to hold against his stomach. "Oh you bugger, that's good. Dan it is then."

"You're gonna have to change that on your own soon I guess?" Chloe ventured.

"Yep, already been shown how to empty it so I'll have to have a go sooner or later."

"You ok with that?" Amy asked, her face full of concern.

"Course, it's just like wiping your arse, except I can have a shit anywhere I like now. Bonus." Josh forced a grin.

"Ooh that's gross, trust you. Did the police come back and question you again?"

"Yeh, twice now and I keep telling them I didn't see the guys who did it but they won't fucking listen." The girls exchanged glances.

"I think they were hoping once the drugs wore off something would come back to you," Chloe ventured tentatively.

"Well it hasn't ok? So let's shut the fuck up about the stabbing shall we girls? Please."

* * *

She put two cups on the table and sat down, drawing her robe tightly around her. "Right, what the fuck is going on?" Her swearing caught him off guard and for a second he hesitated. "Rick?"

"Ok, well...That business with Josh's blood transfusion."

"Did you get that all sorted out then? What happened about that?"

"Oh shit. This would have been so much easier if you had deliberately lied but look at you. You really don't know do you?"

"Know what?"

"It seems...I can't say it," his voice broke with emotion as his eyes filled with tears.

"Rick, just tell me. Whatever it is, just say it. Please," she implored, taking his hands in hers.

"I am not Josh's father," he whispered. "... I AM NOT JOSH'S FATHER!"

Her hands flew to cover her mouth as the color drained from her face leaving her pale and drawn. "That's not possible. You're lying. No I don't believe it. No."

"It's true," he muttered as he choked back a sob. "It's true."

"You are his father, Rick, I swear. You must be...Or else... No, it's impossible."

His head flew up as she rose and began pacing round the table shaking her head muttering "No, no, no."

"What's not possible? Tell me. TELL ME."

"OK! Ok. I had a one night stand two nights before I met you. It was nothing and we used a condom. Before that I hadn't had sex with anyone else for months. After that it was you. I swear. I thought we'd gotten knocked-up real quick but I never imagined it wasn't you. Jesus, Rick I'm so, so sorry. I really had no idea."

She sank back into her chair and burying her face in her hands she began to shake.

He sat for several minutes, sipping his coffee and once the cup was empty he stood up, walked his cup over to the sink and left the house.

CHAPTER 35

"Have either of you seen Lucy lately?"

Amy and Chloe exchanged glances. "Yeh, we see her quite often actually."

He raised his eyebrows, "And?"

"She's good." Chloe nodded.

"Is she...Seeing anyone?"

"Not that I know of."

"How's she doing? I mean really?"

Amy moved to sit on the edge of her brother's bed. "She's trying to make the best of it. She's not looked at anyone else as far as I know. She's not over you yet. Simple as."

He nodded and turned his head to look out of the window. He sniffed and surreptitiously wiped his nose. "Did Dad tell you the whole story?"

"Uh huh," they chorused.

"It's shit in it? The love of my life is my fucking aunt. What are the fucking chances eh?"

"Yes but you went out with Mimi just after Lucy so it can't have been that bad," Chloe whispered. Instantly her brother's head flicked round and he struggled to sit forward in the bed. "You have no fucking idea about me and Lucy or why I moved in with Mimi. Trust me, you have no fucking idea. Ok? Not everything fits into nice little boxes, Chlo', trust me, it really doesn't. I had my heart ripped out and I will never stop caring about Lucy. Understand?"

* * *

"Hi, Elaine."

"Hi, Sal. You ok?"

"Er no, not really. Is Rick with you?"

"Oh...Erm...He was earlier this afternoon. Is everything ok?"

"No I'm really scared, he seems to have disappeared. No stuff's gone, just his car, but he's not answering his phone and no-one's seen him for hours. I've tried the hospital. Franny's. All his mates. Nothing. It's not like him." After several moments Sally heard Elaine's response as if it was coming from a long way away. Her voice sounded strange and distant. Every word seemed a struggle.

"Sal...Something happened today. Something really awful."

"Elaine, you're scaring me."

"Did Rick tell you about Josh's blood transfusion when he was in ITU?"

"Yeh, he said there was a problem with the group and save."

"It wasn't that."

"Eh?"

"... The problem wasn't with the blood it was something else."

"Go on."

"... Rick is not Josh's Dad."

Silence.

"Sally?"

"I'm here. Oh fuck, oh shit. When did he find out?"

"This afternoon, a few hours ago. He was devastated."

"I'M NOT FUCKING SURPRISED!"

"I DIDN'T KNOW EITHER, I swear. I didn't know."

"Don't give me that ole bollocks, how could you not fucking know, Elaine? Were you sleeping around that much you really couldn't tell one from the other. Forgive my lack of sympathy but I think you might just have pushed Rick right over the edge. I'm phoning the police. Might have been nice if you'd told me you'd dropped a bombshell like that into his life. Bit of a heads up would have been useful. Fucking hell. Have you thought to tell Josh by any chance?"

"No, of course not. He doesn't need to know."

"You've got to be joking lady. Isn't that how this whole mess got started? Try telling your son the truth. He might appreciate it and more's the point, he might feel slightly better about having fucked his aunt."

'The other person has cleared, the other person has cleared.' Elaine stared at the phone in her hand for a second then threw it at the wall and watched as it shattered on the floor.

* * *

Sally took his chin and drew his face towards her. She felt the stubble and made a mental note to get him some new razors. He looked back at her pathetically. She smiled back and leant into kiss him. He accepted the kiss but did not respond. "I wondered if you fancied a trip to the restaurant downstairs? For a cuppa and a bit of cake? It's Costa so it's better than the shit they give you up here," she joked. He shrugged. "If you like."

"Well, more to the point it's if you like."

"Don't care," he mumbled.

When she'd found him he'd been out in the rain for over eighteen hours. The police had refused to start a search after such a short period of time and it was Sally who'd eventually discovered him. At first she'd thought he was dead. He was lying on the bench next to his father's grave, stone-cold and un-moving. She'd wrapped him up in her coat and called for the ambulance. After that he'd refused all visitors until she'd crept into his room one night after a late shift and had held him, stroking his hair until he broke down and started talking.

"Ok, if it's my decision then it's coffee downstairs. Where's your dressing gown?"

"I'm not going."

"Oh. Ok babe, no problem." He turned to look out the window again.

* * *

Franny took Sally in her arms and held her for several long minutes before leading her into the sitting room. Giving her time to gather her thoughts, Franny sat silently and patiently. Eventually Sally started to talk. "... It's such a mess. I don't know where to start..."

"Then start with the first thoughts that pop into your head and we'll sort them all out at the end ok?" Sally nodded.

Taking a deep breath she recounted the events of the previous few months. By the time she'd finished she was sobbing softly. "I've lost him, I just can't reach him. No-one can. The psyche team have assessed him and they don't think he's a suicide risk and they've told me to wait until his anti-depressants kick-in but he's not taking 'em now he's home. I found the packet he came home from hospital with, and it was still sealed. He won't see the kids, Elaine, you. He won't even talk to me half the time; he's living like an animal sitting in the dark all day. What the hell am I gonna do, Franny?" The old woman sighed.

"I want you to bring him over here a week from today. In the afternoon. No excuses ok? I have something I want to give him. Right my darling, chin-up. Let's have a drink."

Part 4

CHAPTER 36

Franny held out a folded piece of paper to her nephew and waited for him to take it. He ignored her and stared out of the window. "Richard...Please?" He turned to face her and his eyes were blank and cold. "No thanks, last time you handed me a letter my whole life got ripped apart. Whatever little piece of prose you have in mind that you think will perk me up. Forget it. I'm fine thanks."

"Richard, don't be so bloody arrogant. Take the fucking paper, God knows young man you owe me a little respect after all these years." His eyes flew open and for a second he appeared too stunned to speak. "You swore," he whispered, "I've never heard you swear before."

"Then don't make me swear again. Please, take it." He reached forward and pinched the folded paper between his forefinger and middle finger, making no attempt to open it. "It's a list of people who are important in your life. But the list is divided into two columns. I'm going to put the kettle on and when I come back in with the tea I want you to tell me what the two columns signify ok?" He shrugged. "Oh for God's sake, Richard, indulge me."

"Ok. If I must."

He opened the paper and frowned.

* * *

Elaine Amy
Sally Chloe
Franny Rose
Josh Karen
Jack Sam
Frank Lucy
Eileen Kirsty

Alex   Olly
Ben

* * *

"What the fuck?" He muttered as he frowned at the list. He heard the kettle boil and knew he only had a few minutes to figure out what his aunt was up to. Rubbing his hands over his unshaven face he rotated his shoulders, sat forward and began to think. "Right. It's not gender, age or marital status. Whether they're parents, their professions or location. Shit...How hard can this be? Come on think."

"Do you give up?" She asked smiling as she entered the room carrying the tea-tray. "Have I managed to catch you?"

"No. I just haven't spotted it yet. Can't be that hard surely?" She poured the tea in silence and sat back smugly.

"Ok, I give up." Silently she rose and joined him on the sofa. Taking the paper from him she ran her finger between the lists. "These are all people who care about you. People who are important."

"Yes, you already told me that."

"First a question. Which column do you love the most? Which list of people are most important to you?"

"That's ridiculous. They're all important. I can't say one side or the other."

"Correct. Well, the right-hand column are those that are related to you by blood and the left-hand column are not, but as you've already told me, you love them both the same. There's no difference. Is there?" He raised his eyes to meet hers and smiled.

"That's not fair."

"What's not fair? Pointing out the obvious to someone who's lost their way? Someone you care about who's struggling. Oh darling let me never behave fairly again then."

"Franny...I...I feel like I've lost my history, lost myself. Everything I knew or thought I knew has changed. So many, many lies. It hurts so much."

"Darling, I can't pretend to know how you feel or what it's been like but I know all these people want you in their lives and need you. You don't love Frank and Eileen any less do you, now you know you were adopted?"

"Of course not. I'm upset they lied but I still love them. They're my Mum and Dad."

"Exactly. And Josh? Have you stopped loving him?"

"No way. He's my s...well, he's not is he. But I still love him. I always will but he's probably gonna go off and try and find his real Dad, so I thought I'd respect his wishes and back off."

"You've asked him then?"

"You know I haven't. He doesn't even know yet"

"So why assume you know what he's going to want to do? All the assumptions you've made might explain why Frank and Eileen kept *your* adoption from *you*. You're frightened of losing your son and so were they. See?"

"But...It's not the same...Is it?"

"Isn't it?"

He sat in silence staring at the list. "I've been a complete wanker haven't I?"

She burst out laughing. "Not my choice of words but yes, pretty much. Do you see it now? Really?"

"I think so. Mum and Dad are still Mum and Dad. Josh is still Josh. It still hurts but I think I can start to see a way forward now. I definitely want to get to know Karen and I love having sisters. It's gonna be hard isn't it? To sort all this?"

"Yes. But it will be worth it. Firstly, you need to sort Josh and Lucy out. They both need to know that they're not related. You and Elaine have to tell him, together and please, please, open up to Sally. She's in pieces. She needs some reassurance too."

"Oh shit...Of course, they're not actually related now so they can get back together if they both want to. That's one good thing I guess. Sally...Yeh, I've been a total git haven't I? I love her so much."

"Mmm, well you'd never know it. Don't lose her, Richard. As for Josh and Lucy, well, he needs his Dad and Richard, that's you."

* * *

She heard the taxi pull up outside and felt her throat contract. Daring to peer out the window she saw Rick paying the driver. Her heart lurched as he turned and saw her. For a second he hesitated and then a huge grin spread across his face. Unable to believe her eyes she blinked but his smile remained as he headed for the front door.

"Babe?" He called, throwing his keys onto the hall table. "Sal?"

"In here." He entered the room and walked straight to her. Taking her in his arms he kissed her passionately and deeply and instantly she responded. He crushed her body against his and grabbed her buttocks. She felt him growing hard. Pulling away he held her at arm's-length and looked into her eyes. "Sal, I'm so, so sorry. I've been a total wanker and put you through a really rough time. I just couldn't cope with everything and I know it's not over yet and I'm not completely over the breakdown, but I don't wanna lose you. I love you." She breathed out with a huge sigh. She hadn't even realized she'd been holding her breath. Feeling herself welling up she buried her head in his shoulder and held him tightly.

"Hun? Please, say something. I'm truly sorry. I am. I'll take the meds I promise...Sal?... Sal?" Slowly she lifted her head. Her mascara had run down her cheeks with the tears but she was smiling. He thought she'd never looked more beautiful. "I love you too you silly old fool." He smiled down at her, took her hand and started to lead her upstairs.

"Are you sure about this, Rick? I mean...You still seem a bit...Well, fragile...Don't do this for me." He placed a finger on her lips to silence her.

"It's not for you, it's for us. Fran put me straight on a few things and in the taxi home I realized the last time

I'd felt truly safe, grounded and happy was making love to you. We've always had this rule about shutting the door and shutting the world out. We have that for a very good reason. I need you and I need to feel safe and happy. You give me that. This isn't about having an orgasm it's about making love. Indulge me. Please." She smiled and leant up to kiss him again. As she leant into him she felt his hard-on straining against his flies. "Seems like you and little brain there are way ahead of me." He laughed.

"Better give you a chance to catch up then."

He ran his fingers down her throat, towards her breasts. She closed her eyes. "Take it off," he whispered and she slid her t-shirt up over her head. Before she could lower her arms he held them above her head and placed his mouth over her nipple and started to suck her already hard nub through the lacy fabric. The sensation was like an electric current surging through her body and she responded by arching her back and pushing her breast towards his mouth. Biting the lace carefully he pulled at her.

Holding both her hands in one he brought his free hand down to her bra and casually slipped a finger into the cup, pulling the fabric down to release her breast. She moaned softly as she felt her clitoris tingle.

Her eyes flew open. "Oh shit...Rick, no. We can't...Shit I just remembered. I'm on. Bollocks."

"OK. No problem," he replied casually as he resumed teasing her with his tongue.

"What does that mean?"

"I don't care. I love you, I want you. I'm a nurse. I don't get freaked out by a little blood. It'll be fine. I'll put a towel on the bed."

"Really?... You're sure?" He laughed and planted a small peck on the tip of her nose.

"Absolutely. Now where were we? Oh, yes."

His teeth grazed her nipple as he softly nibbled at her. Letting her hands go, his arms drifted behind her and in a second her bra floated to the floor. "Let's get comfy," he whispered as he led her to the bed and laid her down. Kneeling over her undid her jeans and slid them down her thighs. As he caught sight of her he felt his breath catch in his throat.

He ran his fingers up the insides of her thighs and felt her quiver in response. Her eyes were closed, her head thrown back and she was gripping the quilt in both hands. Using only his fingertips he eased her briefs down over her hips. "Lift up, babe." Instantly she sat up. "I need the bathroom first. I have a tampon in."

"No you don't. Stay where you are. Relax, shush. Lay back and lift up." She frowned.

"What about your bed linen?"

"Who cares? I don't." Hesitating for only a second she resumed her position and he slid her underwear off.

Spreading her thighs with his palms he traced her delicate, pink lips with his fingers. Her clitoris was already hard and glistened at him, moist and sensuous and he longed to make her come. "I'm gonna take the tampon out ok?"

"No! I'll do it."

"No. I'll do it. Ok?"

"Ok. Jeez, in for a penny in for a pound I guess. You are one kinky bastard."

He smiled at her as he eased the tampon from her body and dropped it onto her pants on the floor, beside the bed. She gasped. "I am so turned on right now." He grinned at her.

"Me too."

Looking at her glistening pink pussy he leant in and softly kissed her inner thighs, she shivered and moaned. "Just relax babe." His finger stroked the length of her lips, casually brushing against her clitoris, instantly she bucked off the bed. As her hips rose up he slid a finger into the hot depths and felt her shudder in response. She felt hotter and wetter than she'd ever felt before. A second and then a third finger slipped into her and as he nudged her clitoris with his thumb he felt her fanny tighten around his hand as she worked herself against his fingers. She was soaking wet and about to come and he felt himself rushing headlong towards his own climax. "Oh shit, I'm so close," he murmured. "Hang on, give me a minute."

"Fuck me, now, please. I want you inside me," she panted.

"You're sure?"

"Holy shit, yes. Please...Oh God I'm gonna come. Oh God!"

"Shit I still have my jeans on. Hang on."

"Oh what? Hurry up."

Frantically he freed himself from his jeans and boxers and knelt between her knees as they gazed into each other's eyes. She was flushed, her nipples were hard, her hair was tangled and disheveled and her pussy was wet. "You've never looked more gorgeous. I love you."

"I love you too," she panted, "but if you don't get inside me I may spontaneously combust." He smiled and as he approached her she reached down and began to stroke her delicate folds. He eased into her slowly and then pulled out, each time almost removing his cock from her but pushing in further and harder each time. Within seconds he felt her hips rock as she thrust against him, forcing his cock into her hard and deep. She grabbed his arse and rammed his body against hers to get maximum depth to each thrust. Her orgasm was intense and he pushed her hand away and rubbed her little pink nub as he filled her until he too lost control and let himself come with her. Together they thrust against each other in an intense climax that left them both exhausted.

He collapsed on top of her and kissed her forehead, nose, lips and nipples. "That was incredible...Oh hun, what's wrong?" He looked at the tears in her eyes and instantly panicked. "Have I hurt you? Oh shit, was I too rough?" She laughed up at him.

"No, you idiot, I'm just so happy. These are tears of happiness. I love you but for a while I thought I'd lost you. You seemed so distant. It was horrible. Welcome back."

"It's nice to be back. Franny taught me really simple lesson. You love the people you love not because they're related to you but because of who they are."

"Is that it?"

"Yep, she gave me a list of people's names divided into two columns and I had to guess what the two categories were. It turns out it was blood relatives and non blood relatives but before she told me she asked me which group meant the most. Who I loved best and, of course, I loved both groups the same and that's when she told me. Clever huh?"

"She's a wiley old bird that one."

"Yes. She is, I'm lucky to have her...Sal. I need to ask you something."

"Ok, go ahead."

"... Will you marry me?"

"What?... What did you say?" He grinned at her.

"You heard me."

"Really? Seriously? Of course."

CHAPTER 37

"Josh we need to talk to you."

"Shit, last time you said that the brown stuff hit the fan and my life got completely fucked up." Elaine glanced at Rick and swallowed hard. Her heart was thumping in her chest and she felt a little faint and nauseous. Rick smiled reassuringly and gave her the merest hint of a nod. She took a deep breath and turned to her son.

"I know. I'm truly sorry. You've had such a terrible time recently but there's something we need to tell you." Josh sighed, rubbed his hands over his face and leant back in the chair. That gesture is so like Rick, Elaine thought, the irony making her grimace. "Ok, whatever it is you'd better get it out 'cause ma, you look like you're gonna explode if you don't." All three laughed and for second the tension eased. She turned to her ex-husband.

"Quick or slow? Rick, you say."

"Quick. Like a plaster." She nodded just once.

"Ok, here goes. Josh, your Dad is not..." Her voice faded away as her tears caught in her throat. "He's not...Oh, Rick, I can't say the words. I'm sorry." Rick took a deep breath, stood up and turned towards the window so his face was hidden.

"I'm not your biological father. The blood tests at the hospital have proved it. Mum didn't cheat or anything. She had a one night stand the week we met, she used a condom but she must have already conceived by the time we started sleeping together. I love you but you're not technically my son. That's it."

Silence.

Rick lifted his head. Josh's face was white and his mouth was hanging open. Slowly a smile spread across his face. "You buggers! That's a sick joke, even for you two."

"Josh, please, Dad's serious. It was the thought of losing you that caused his breakdown. Telling you is possibly the hardest thing he's ever done." Josh started to shake his head.

"No way. It's not true. It can't be." Rick sat down next to Josh and took his hands in his own.

"Joshua, I love you and you will always be my son. Blood or no blood. Nothing's changed for me. I promise you. Telling lies and keeping secrets has cost this family dearly so I wanted you to know the truth and if you wanna look for your natural father that's fine. I'll support you all the way." Josh stared at their hands intertwined and was suddenly drawn back to all the times his father had held him up over the years. When he'd tripped over, when he'd had chicken pox, when he'd fallen off the swing and had needed stitches, when he'd learnt to ride his bike and when he'd woken up in ITU his Dad's face had been the first he'd seen. A huge sobbed escaped him as his tears fell. "Dad...I...You're my Dad...That's it. End of...I don't know what I'd do without you. You're my mate and I love you. Thanks for telling me," he turned to include his mother and saw that she too was crying. "Both of you, and I appreciate your honesty but it changes nothing." Within seconds all three were hugging each other and crying.

After what seemed like an eternity Rick cleared his throat and took a deep breath. "There's one more thing. This means that you and Lucy are free to get back together. If you want to that is?"

Josh frowned. "Lucy...Jesus...Yes of course. We're not actually related now are we?"

"Josh, honey, do you still have feelings for her?"

"Mum, she's the love of my life. I adore her and always will, but so much time has passed I don't know if she still cares about me."

"You'd better find out then hadn't you? She's at Dad's waiting for you."

His face split into a huge grin. "What?... Really? Shit, can you drive me please?"

"Of course."

Suddenly her son's face darkened, "Does she know about Dan?"

"Dan?... Oh your stoma? Yes Dad's talked to her. She's totally cool with it. Turns out her best friend Kelly's Mum has one."

"Really?" Josh frowned.

"I know, how spooky is that? Come on, grab your stuff."

"But has she actually seen one? Does she really know what it really means to have one?"

Rick took Josh by the shoulders. "Josh, if she had one would it change how you feel about her?"

"Of course not."

"Well then. You love her and she loves you. You'll work it out."

"But what if..."

"Josh, son, you won't know until you give it a try. We've talked about it and I know she understands, probably more than most people. Trust me, she's fine about it." Josh nodded and forced a smile. His hands shook as he fumbled with his seat belt as he tried to imagine exposing his body to anyone let alone having sex again.

* * *

Lucy wiped her palms down her jeans for the umpteenth time and checked her watch. Her heart was pounding and her mouth felt dry. She took a large sip of her water but it didn't help. "How much longer?" She muttered. Making her way to the bathroom she locked the door and sat down. As soon as she did she heard the front door open. "Oh bollocks," she mumbled as she struggled to pull up her jeans.

"Luce...LUCY?" He heard the toilet flush and let out a sigh of relief. He was sure she'd changed her mind.

He stood in the hall and smiled up at her as she came down the stairs. She grinned back at him. They were both close to tears and unable to speak. Without hesitation she walked into his arms and as their lips connected she knew she'd come home.

CHAPTER 38

Sally and Rick stood hand in hand at the door and took a second to exchange looks before ringing the bell.

If Jack was surprised to see them, he hid it well. "Hello there. Nice to see you both. Come on in. Karen's in the kitchen. Go straight through. Fancy a cuppa?"

"Thanks, Jack. That would be really nice. Ta."

Karen was standing with her back to the room, stirring a pan on the hob. "Who was it love? Anyone important."

"You could say that," Rick replied grinning sheepishly. Instantly she spun round, her eyes wide, her mouth hanging open. "Close your mouth girl, there's a bus coming," Jack teased. Rick smiled over at him.

"I'm gonna stick the kettle on. You'd better all sit down, you especially, Ka. You look like you're gonna bloody fall down. Now, tea or coffee?"

* * *

Josh took her hand and led her into the lounge. "Do you mind if we sit for a minute. I still get a bit tired." Her face contorted with concern as she leant forward to look deep into his eyes. "I heard all about the stabbing. My Dad told me. Oh, babe, I can't believe you nearly died. I've been so worried. If they ever catch who did it I'll..."

"They won't. Trust me, they won't. Anyway, it wasn't that bad really."

"Stop it...Stop it," her voice cracked with emotion. "I know how bad it was. Your Dad kept me up to date and I came to see you."

"What?"

She smiled. "When you were sedated in ITU. I couldn't bear it. You looked so fragile with all those tubes. I came very day until they told me you were well enough to move to the ward. Then I just got Rick to keep me up to date." He stared at her, astonished, unable to speak, imagining her watching over him.

"But...How come I didn't know...Why didn't anyone tell me?" Placing a soft kiss on his lips she ran a hand down his cheek and cupped his face. "I just wanted to see you, in case...Well, you know, in case you didn't make it. I was so scared, they couldn't have kept me away if they'd tried. I thought that if you saw me it would make things worse. I didn't know what to do. I just knew I had to see you." He nodded and turned his face to plant a kiss on her palm. She smiled back at him.

"Kiss me," he whispered and as she leant in to kiss him their tongue's met and as the kiss deepened both felt the unbearable urge to touch and rediscover each other.

Josh nibbled at her lips as his hand drifted towards her soft breasts. Her nipples were already hard and he became aware that she was bra-less. "Ooh nice." She giggled in response as he slid her t-shirt over her head. Running his hands over her he teased her nipples with little kisses and nips making her moan and squirm. He felt his cock straining against his jeans and longed for her to free him and take him in her mouth. He remembered the evening in the car when she'd done just that and instantly he felt the all too familiar wave approaching as he struggled not to come. "Take your top off," she urged. For a second he moved to remove the shirt when suddenly he realized.

"NO!"

"Josh? What's wrong?"

At that moment his stoma farted and his erection disappeared. He pushed her off and stormed from the room leaving her exposed, hurt and confused. She heard his bedroom door slam as she buried her face in her hands.

* * *

"Oh shit, we're out of milk. Sal, fancy a walk down the shop with me?" Before Sally could answer Karen stood up and placed both hands on her hips.

"We're not out of milk, Jack," Karen argued as she made her way to the fridge. Jack moved to block her way. "WE *ARE* OUT OF MILK AND SALLY AND I ARE GOING TO GET SOME. OK?" She sighed as Sally and Rick smiled at each other.

"Jack, what the hell are you playing at?"

"Ka, just sit down will ya. Rick, we'll walk the long way back ok?"

"Cheers, Jack. Appreciate it mate."

They sat in silence as the back door closed. After several minutes Rick stood up and got some milk from the fridge and continued with the tea. "Stupid old man," she muttered, "did he really think we believed that story about the milk?"

"No, course not, but I appreciate the effort. He's a nice bloke. You're lucky to have him."

"I know. I've always known. He is a nice bloke and a great Dad. That was part of the problem to be honest."

"How come?" He said as he placed two mugs on the table and sat down.

"He's so nice and such a good husband and a good Dad I could never bring myself to tell him about you. I knew what would happen and it didn't seem fair. I never imagined Frank and Eileen would tell you about me. Never. They wanted to be sure I never came after you so I assumed they'd keep the secret."

"They did. For forty-three years. Still amazes me that so many people kept their mouths shut. Mum wrote the letter years ago but made Franny promise to keep it until she died."

"I can't decide whether I think that was a good idea or not. Seems a bit unfair leaving you to deal with all this on your own. I can't believe you found me either, and as for you and Jack working in the same hospital. That beggars belief."

"I know. But my main concern is Josh and Lucy."

"How is he now he's home?"

"He's fine. Yeh doing well. I have something to tell you about Josh and it concerns Lucy too."

"Ok."

"I found out by accident that Josh is not my son..."

"WHAT?"

"Yeh."

She tentatively placed a hand over his. "Rick, I'm so, so sorry. That must have been a terrible shock."

"Yeh, you could say that. Turns out Elaine was already pregnant when we met but didn't know it. It was as much of a shock to her as it was to me."

"Really?"

"Yeh, I could tell by her face that she was telling me the truth. Anyway, we've told Josh and of course that means that he and Lucy..."

"... Can get back together again." A huge smile spread across her face. "That's great news, does she know?"

"Yep, in fact, they're together at mine as we speak."

CHAPTER 39

"Josh, JOSH! Open the door, please."

"Lucy, just go will ya. This isn't gonna work. I'm sorry." She heard him stifle a sob through the bedroom door.

"OPEN THIS FUCKING DOOR!" She screamed. Silence. "JOSH, I'M NOT LEAVING AND I *WILL* STAND HERE AND SCREAM ALL DAY!"

She heard the key turn in the lock but the door remained shut. Slowly she turned the handle and opened the door. The bedroom was empty but the door to the en-suite was closed. "Oh for fuck's sake. You're running out of doors. Will you please just talk to me? At least tell me what just happened. You owe me that at least."

Slowly the door opened and Josh stood in front of her totally naked. "THIS," he shouted pointing to his stoma. "THIS IS WHAT HAPPENED. I HAVE A FUCKING SACK OF SHIT STRAPPED TO MY BODY TWENTY FOUR HOURS A DAY. IT FARTS, IT SHITS, AND IT STINKS AND THERE'S NOT A FUCKING THING I CAN DO ABOUT IT." Despite his formidable size he looked nothing more than a frightened little boy.

"I know about Dan," she replied quietly.

"You think you do but you really don't. Look at me. Just look. It's revolting. I wouldn't ask anyone to spend time with it especially..."

"Especially?"

"Especially someone I love the way I love you," he whispered.

"How dare you?" Her anger took him by surprise.

"What?"

"How dare you presume to know my mind better than I do? How dare you make choices for me? How dare you tell me what I think about your stoma when you haven't even had the decency to ask me?"

"Lucy...?"

"No, Josh. You have a stoma. So what? I don't give a shit...No pun intended...But I don't. You really think I'm that shallow?"

"It's not that..."

"I fancy you with, or without Dan. I love you with, or without Dan. I thought I'd lost you and now I have the chance to get you back and you're letting a sack of shit - your words not mine -, keep us apart. I thought you loved me."

Slowly he walked towards her. "I love you more than life itself. I always will. I just thought..."

"I can't believe you'd give up without a fight. It's nothing. It's a stoma. Really. It's not who you are it's something that happened to you. I love you. Don't you dare use Dan as an excuse to push me away."

He took her hands in his. "I was trying to give you the chance to walk away. Guilt free. I would understand if you did. I hate Dan. It's embarrassing. I'm ashamed of how I look and I never wanted you to see me like this."

"You're such a dick! You're as gorgeous and sexy as ever. I have no intention of walking away. Why? Do you?"

"Hell no. When I was in ITU I dreamt I was making love to you. It's the only thing I remember."

His erection nudged her stomach and she rubbed against it. "Looks like you remember it really well," she teased.

He smiled sheepishly. "You're all I've thought about for so long. Your lips. Your body. Touching you. Licking you. Being inside you. Making love to you. I want you so bad."

"So, what's stopping you?"

"You're sure?"

"If I was gonna run I wouldn't be here now and besides, I'm wet and horny. This is long overdue. Come, lay down with me, please."

* * *

He sipped his tea and raised his eyes. She was looking at him intently. She blushed. "I'm sorry. It's just that you're so like your Dad."

"S'ok. I understand. That's the other thing I want to talk about. Jack told me about the whole set-up with Rose. How she told him the truth about you and the adoption. I wanted to say I finally understand. After I met Rose I knew it was the truth. She's a formidable character and I can't imagine contradicting her now, let alone as a pregnant fifteen year old."

She laughed. "You've got that right."

"I need to ask you something."

"Ok."

"Do we have a future, you and me? Is it gonna be polite small talk at family occasions or do we have a chance to have a real relationship?"

She leant back in the chair and stared at the ceiling. "What do *you* want?"

"Me? Isn't that obvious? I was the one who wanted to find you, remember?"

"Of course. So you still want us to be...What?... Friends?... Mother and son?"

"I'd settle for friends and see what happens. Eileen will always be Mum but I'd like us to have something special."

She turned and met his gaze again. They both had tears in their eyes.

* * *

They lay naked, side by side on the bed. As Josh's tongue traced the shape of her nipples she closed her eyes and moaned softly. He dragged a finger the length of her stomach and as he delicately grazed her pubes she rolled onto her back. Sliding a finger between her lips he found her already soaking wet and gorgeously hot. His kisses traced a line down her stomach and as he spread her thighs he buried his face in her pussy. The sweet fragrance of her, the heat, the delicious moistness. So very gently he lapped at her clitoris as he teased her open with his fingers. Spreading her legs wider she lifted her bottom from the mattress and rubbed herself against him. He took her arse in his hands and as he thrust his tongue into her tight little minge he spread her wide and tickled her arse with his fingers. Within seconds her panting became faster and he felt her pussy throbbing around his tongue. Instantly she began to rock against him as she came over and over. The taste of her almost carrying him to climax. "Fuck me," she panted.

Needing no further instructions he rolled her over and lifted her up. As he nudged her knees apart he glimpsed her delicate folds and her glistening, hot little minge between her gorgeous arse cheeks and he bent down to lap at her one more time, she giggled with surprise and instantly started to come again. Sliding into her inch by inch he felt her hips thrusting against him as her pussy pulsated around him, gripping his cock. She was so beautifully tight. He knew he was only seconds away. Her hand reached for her clitoris and as her orgasm intensified he relaxed and let himself pump hard into her.

CHAPTER 40

Six Months Later

Karen opened the photograph album lying in her lap and wiped her eyes for the umpteenth time. Each photo made her both smile and cry.

She turned to the first page again and admired her son and grandson standing outside the church. Rick looked so like Sam and for a brief moment she allowed herself to imagine what their wedding might have been like.

The second page showed her gorgeous granddaughters; Amy and Chloe in their beautiful coffee colored bridesmaid's dresses that perfectly complimented their mixed-race coloring. She sniffed loudly.

The next page showed Sally and her Dad waiting to go into the church. Her daughter-in-law looked radiant in her beautiful ivory gown.

Flicking to the back of the album she turned to the pages with the groups and smiled at her family. Lucy, six months pregnant and blooming, Kirsty, Alex and the twins; Olly and Ben in their cute little suits. Rose, grinning from ear to ear with pride. And finally her and Jack. Holding hands and beaming. Unable to hold back the tears she started sobbing again.

Walking into the room Jack frowned. "Oh love, not again. What are you bloody like?" She smiled guiltily. "I know, but I can't help it. It was such a beautiful wedding. They all looked so lovely. My family. I'm so proud of them all. From the day he was born I never imagined I'd ever get to see him let alone be at his wedding. I'm so lucky."

"I know, you daft ole mare. Right. You ready?"

"Yeh, just let me put the photos away."

* * *

196

She picked up the vase of dead flowers and emptied them into the dustbin. Filling the vase with clean water she arranged the blooms and stood it on the grave. Sam's headstone was worn and old, and reading the date caused her to reflect on how many years he'd been gone. She swallowed hard. Jack slipped a hand into hers. "Alright?"

"Mmm."

"Come on then."

They walked in silence to the next row of graves.

She gazed at the names through her tears; Frank Arthur Murphy and Eileen Mary Murphy. She placed a second bunch of flowers on their grave and smiled as she kissed her fingers and placed them softly against the stone.

"Thank you both for looking after him. I promise I'll do my best to keep them all safe from now on," she whispered.

Lightning Source UK Ltd.
Milton Keynes UK
UKOW04f0708141214

243063UK00002B/143/P